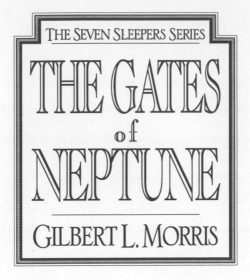

THE SEVEN SLEEPERS SERIES

THE GATES of NEPTUNE

GILBERT L. MORRIS

MOODY PRESS

CHICAGO

ISBN: 0-8024-3682-X

10

Printed in the United States of America

TO THE O'KEEFE KIDS—

Eran   Asher
Oshea   Urias
Isaac

*May you all grow up to be as
fine and dedicated as you are now!*

Contents

1

Out of the Frying Pan

The great stone door swung slowly to and fell into place with a click.

"Quick," Josh urged, "they're coming!"

Even as he spoke, the angry cries of the soldiers of the Sanhedrin sounded, and they began to pound on the stone walls.

At his side, Sarah shivered. "We just barely made it, didn't we, Josh?"

"Yes. Inside, right now!" Calling their names, tall, lean, freckled Josh shoved his companions in quickly, pushing them one by one down the corridor that led to a gentle, downhill slope. "We've got to get away. They may break through the door."

The company that made its way down through the dark passageway, lit only by torches at irregular intervals, was strange indeed. Sarah watched the group in front of her, thinking, *I never thought to see such creatures as these—not on this earth.* But she knew she was not on the old earth. She was on a planet completely changed by nuclear war. The changes had brought genetic transformation, so that Oldworld was gone and now new sub-species were to be seen.

She glanced again at the group ahead, those members of the new world who had been chosen to help keep the Seven Sleepers from the wrath of the Sanhedrin. Three of them were the strange looking "hunters"—one having huge eyes that could see, it seemed, forever; the second having great ears that flopped and wiggled; and the third having a large, twitching nose, so that together the three made what was called the Hunter.

Next in line was the giant, Volka, larger than any human had ever been on earth. He had powerful, bulky muscles and a blunt but kind face. Then came two sets of twins, "Gemini twins," who had to stay close together all their lives—Mat and Tam, and the females Amar and Rama. If they were separated, Sarah knew, they would die. And last came their friend Kybus.

"Look! There are some boats," Jake called out. His red hair shone in the light of the torches. "Five of them. How did they know how many boats we'd need?"

"We can worry about that later," Josh said. "Let's get aboard."

One boat was required for the giant. The twins got in another, and Kybus and the Hunter in the next.

"Sarah, you, Reb, and Wash go with me," Josh said. "Dave, you take Abbey, and Jake."

"Right," Dave said.

And they began to climb into the small, flimsy-looking boats.

"Wow," Reb said, his pale blue eyes staring doubtfully at the little craft. "I wouldn't go fishing on the Mississippi in a thing like this."

"It's what we have," Josh said impatiently. "The Sleepers will bring up the rear. The rest of you, go on."

"Yes," Kybus said, his sharp face glowing with intelligence. "Come. I've got the feeling that we need to hurry. They have ways of breaking through stone walls."

The first three boats shoved off, then Dave, Abbey, and Jake followed. Sarah sat down between Reb and Wash, and Josh took the stern, handling the paddle.

The current was swift, and Wash said, "I sure hope that this don't get fast. I can't swim a lick. Can the rest of you?"

As it turned out, Josh was the only one who could swim well, but he said, "Don't worry, this is easy. I've done a lot of canoeing, and if the current doesn't get any faster than this, we're all right."

They glided along smoothly. The underground stream was black in the darkness. Only their hand-held torches cast reflections.

Somehow Sarah sensed that this was a very deep river. She had never liked boating—or water—and since she was not much of a swimmer, fear ran over her. But she said nothing.

They had glided along for perhaps half an hour when Josh said, "I think the current's getting faster." He called ahead, "How is it up there?"

From far in front came the voice of Kybus, very faint, "Be careful, be careful."

"I don't like this." Wash's black face was tense, and his usual cheerful smile was gone. He clung to the sides of the boat. "Sure wish we could get out in the open."

Reb, perhaps trying to lighten the situation, said, "You know what this is like?"

"I know it's like something weird," Sarah said. "What's it like to you, Reb?"

"Why, I went in one of them parks in Dallas, and they had a thing called the Log Ride. I got into that sucker and slid down all the way. And you know what?—it was fun!"

Josh said, "I've been there too, and it *was* fun, but this is a little different." Suddenly he cried out, "Look, look up there!"

Sarah looked up and saw at once what he had seen.

"The ceiling's getting lower," Josh said.

Far ahead, they heard a cry, and a cold chill ran down Sarah's back. Not only was the river beginning to boil, throwing forward the little boats at a speed that was terrifying, but was the ceiling closing in on them? Before, it had been high enough so that their torches barely illuminated it, but now she saw that it was only a few feet above their heads.

"What if it plays out?" Reb asked suddenly. "What'll we do then?"

"Never happen," Josh said.

But was he feeling queasy himself? Sarah wondered. Was his stomach churning too? This closing in of the ceiling and the racing of the river were things he must have never counted on.

But Josh said, "We'll be all right."

Another cry came from far ahead. "Look out!" And then silence.

"The tunnel's closing in!" Sarah cried. Now the ceiling was so close that she could almost reach up and touch it. "We're all going to drown!"

Sarah grabbed at Josh. She caught his arm, which he was using to paddle, and caused him to miss a stroke.

He said angrily, "Don't hold onto me, Sarah. I need to guide the boat."

As if they hadn't enough trouble, suddenly the torches far ahead of them disappeared—just flickered out, except for the one right in front containing the other Sleepers. "Are you all right?" Josh cried out. "Dave?"

Dave's voice floated back. "We're all right, but it looks like we're running out of river. I can't even see the others."

The ceiling dropped lower and lower, and now it was as if the boat were being drawn into a giant whirlpool. The water was white. Its roaring as it streamed over the rocks was almost deafening. The fury of the rushing water and the sensation of being closed in were terrifying. Fear rose to grip Sarah, and then she heard Abigail scream.

"We're all going to die! We're all going to die!"

And at that moment, though she had little use for Abigail's manners, Sarah thought there was some excuse for the girl's terror.

"Hang on, hang on!" Josh said. "We'll make it."

There was a mighty roar then as the river seemed to reach a crescendo of sound, and Sarah gave up all hope. She crouched in the bottom of the boat, covered her ears with her hands, and began crying out to Goel for help.

And then, as if in answer to her cry, the roaring began to diminish. Sarah looked up to see that the ceiling was no longer right above her head but was rising—almost magically, it seemed.

"We made it through! We made it through!" Josh cried. "Look ahead there!"

Sarah gasped in amazement. They had come into a huge cavern with a ceiling so high that it seemed to go up forever. The torches did not enable them even to see it. On each side, they began to pass huge stalactites and stalagmites that glittered like diamonds, reflecting the torchlight.

"We've come to a big cave," Sarah cried out. "Oh, Josh, there's a shore over there. Let's land on it, quick."

"I think that's a good idea." Josh called out, "Dave, see that shore? I think we'd better pull in."

"All right," Dave called back.

The two boats turned toward a long, sloping beach in a side eddy of the river. As the first boat landed, Jake leaped out and pulled in the prow. Reb did the same for the second boat.

Soon everyone was out on the sand, and Reb was lighting other torches so that they could see what sort of place they were in.

"Why it's like Mammoth Cave," Sarah said. "I was there one time. It looked like this."

"Well, I'm just glad to be anywhere," Jake said. "I thought we'd had it back in that river." He looked all around. "Where are the Nuworlders?"

Dave said, "Didn't you see that divide back there?"

"No, I didn't see anything," Josh said. "What was it?"

"The river divided, and the other boats went the other way. I didn't have a chance to even make a choice—it just seemed like this branch sucked us into it."

Sarah looked around, saw the pale faces, and knew that her own was no better. Everybody's nerves seemed a little shaky. "Let's fix something to eat," she said. "Then we can talk about what we are going to do."

That idea sounded good to the others, and soon they were busy preparing a meal.

"Someone had planned for us," Reb said as he pulled food and firewood out of the boat. "I don't know what kind of grub this is, but I'll be glad to have it."

As the others prepared the food, Josh went up and down the beach. He came back just when the meal was ready. "Well, we might as well eat, because we're sure not going but one way."

They sat down and ate the meat, which was delicious, and afterwards Wash asked, "Well, what are we going to do now?"

Dave shrugged uncertainly. He was a tall, handsome boy of fifteen, the oldest of the group. He had fine, yellow hair and striking blue eyes. "Not much choice about that. We're separated from the rest, and we can't go back up the river, can we?"

"No," Sarah said at once. She was fourteen, small, graceful, very pretty. Her black hair was now wet with the spray of the river. She said, "But we're all right. Goel has brought us this far."

It was Abigail Roberts, who at thirteen was the most attractive of the Sleepers, beautiful, blue-eyed, blonde-haired, very small and well-shaped, and yet always complaining, who said, "No, we're all going to die down here." She pouted. "We'll never get out."

Jake shook his head stubbornly. "Goel didn't save us to let us die like moles underground."

The argument went on for some time, but at last it was obvious to everyone, even seemingly to Abigail, that they were going to have to go on down the river.

Reb summed it up. "Well, I'll tell you, back in the war, Stonewall Jackson, when he seen a bunch of Yankees, he always done one thing."

"What was that, Reb?"

"Why, he charged 'em!" Reb exclaimed. He waved his hand toward the stream. "And we're going to do exactly the same thing." He had pale, sun-bleached hair and light blue eyes, as had his ancestors on the fields of Bull Run and Antietam. "And we'll do it too! But first, I think I'm going to rest a while."

Everyone seemed exhausted. They found blankets in the bottom of the boats—a little soggy but better than nothing, and it was not freezing in the cave. They lay down wearily, and soon most of them were asleep.

But Sarah lay awake for a long time. She was thinking about all the things that had brought the seven of them to this place, and now she began to think of the strange person called Goel, who appeared from time to time to give them counsel.

"Who is he?" she whispered. "*What* is he, and why do I believe in him so much?" But she knew that Goel, whoever or whatever he was, had proven himself to be their friend. "So," she said, as she began to drop off to sleep, "I'll trust him. You have to trust somebody, so I'll trust him."

She was almost asleep when suddenly her eyes flew open. She had heard splashing out on the smooth water, and then a footstep.

"Josh—wake up! Somebody's coming."

Josh, lying close by, came awake instantly. "What is it?"

"Somebody's coming."

Josh quickly awakened the others, and they gathered in a group as a shadowy shape moved toward them.

Josh said, "There's just one. Come on, you guys, let's get him."

As they charged across the sandy beach, Reb let out a wild rebel cry that almost raised the hair on the back of Sarah's neck. Reb got to the intruder first and threw himself on him. Down they went. The others were yelling and trying to get into the fight. Then Sarah ran up holding a torch, saying, "Who are you?"

Josh grabbed an arm, jerked the intruder to his feet, and then stood stock still. A gasp went up from the group, and Josh muttered, "Why—you're just a girl!"

What Sarah saw was a young woman of perhaps eighteen, with black hair and green eyes. She wore some sort of transparent costume through which Sarah could see a green swimming suit that looked much like fish scales. A strange-looking belt was around her waist, having several tubes that ran up to the top of her suit.

"My name is Jere," she said quietly. "And Goel has sent me to be your guide."

Silence fell over the Sleepers. They stared wildly at one another, and then looked again carefully at the beautiful young woman.

"Well," Sarah said tartly, "if there's a pretty girl in a hundred miles, you'll find her, won't you, Josh?"

2
Friend—or Foe?

Josh shot a startled look at Sarah, then shook his head in disgust, but made no answer. Instead, he looked at the young woman and said harshly, "We'll have to know a little bit more about you than that before we follow you anywhere."

The young woman called Jere turned to Josh. She seemed able to make quick decisions, and apparently she had decided that Josh was the leader here. When she spoke again, her voice was low and pleasant, and her green eyes caught the flicker of the torches.

"I think you are wise to question me," she said. "These are not normal days, and one does not know, at times, who is a friend and who is a foe."

Dave stepped forward, his chin held out defiantly. "Well, prove it to us, then—which one you are, a friend or a foe."

"I cannot do that."

The Sleepers glanced at each other again. Sarah knew she was not satisfied with this reply.

Reb Jackson shoved his cowboy hat back on his head and said carefully, "Well, shoot. Here you are, a strange young lady who popped up out of a river wearing a garb like I've never seen before, and you want us to follow you blind."

Jere nodded, and a slight smile turned up the corners of her lips. "I'm afraid that's the way it must be," she said calmly.

Josh looked upset. This was another of those crises

that seemed to tear the group apart at times. As close as they had grown during their dangerous adventures together, still they were seven strong-minded young people. "Do you know who we are?" he asked finally.

"No," Jere answered, shaking her head. Her hair was cut short and was a mass of curls, and she looked very pretty standing before them. She was small, but strongly built, like a swimmer or a gymnast. "I know nothing about you except that Goel sent me to bring you to your destination." She looked at them curiously. "I might ask the same of you as you of me. Who *are* you, and why would Goel want you to come to my home?"

Something about the young woman pleased Sarah. "You really don't know who we are?"

"No. You look like a group of young people, obviously out of Oldtime. Who are you, and what are you doing in this cave?"

Sarah glanced around. "It may save time if I tell her." Without waiting, she plunged into an explanation. "We all come from Oldworld," she said quickly. "Before the great war, which destroyed the old world, we were all placed in what you might call time capsules. We stayed there—asleep—until the war was over and for long afterwards. But finally we were awakened, and all came together. We only know that somehow we're going to be used to bring Nuworld to a time of peace, and we think," she added, "that Goel is the key to that."

Jere had listened carefully. Finally she gave a deep sigh and ran her hands restlessly over her hair. She shook her head sadly. "Peace, what we all long for, but what most of us never find." Then she straightened up and seemed to be thinking. "Well, obviously I cannot force you to go with me. You will have to decide. I will go down the beach and wait while you talk among yourselves."

Without another word, the young woman walked away.

16

As soon as she was out of hearing distance, Dave said, "I don't know about this. She could be anybody. How do we know she's not one of the Sanhedrin's spies?"

Abigail said, "But she doesn't look like a spy. She's too pretty for that."

Jake Garfield grinned, his red hair over his eyes. "Well, sometimes I think it's better for spies to be pretty—get more sympathy that way."

Reb said, "Shoot, I don't know. Here she appears in the middle of nowhere and says we're supposed to follow her." His eyes were troubled, and though he had courage enough for ten young men, something about blindly following a woman clearly bothered him.

The talk went on for some time until finally Josh said, "We can't stand here arguing. We'll have to vote. Everybody that's in favor of following Jere to wherever she takes us, hold up your hand." When he looked around, every hand was up except Dave's and Reb's.

"Well," Josh said, "you two will just have to go along, I guess. Majority rules." He lifted his head and called out, "Jere—Jere."

The young woman came back up the beach. "Have you made up your mind?"

"Yes. Some of us aren't sure, but we're going to trust you. But I warn you," he said suddenly, "if anything goes wrong, I'll be very close to you." He pulled a knife out of his belt. "I don't want to sound unkind—but something may happen to you."

Jere smiled suddenly, and she had one of those smiles where the eyes crinkle up until they're almost invisible. She laughed aloud. "You are wise beyond your years, young man. Come along, and I will take you to your destination."

"You ride in the boat with me," Josh said.

"No. You all will follow me."

There was something majestic about her manner. As she walked toward the boats, Jake said, "I don't know who she is, but whoever she is, she's *somebody!*"

The others seemed to agree, even Reb and Dave. They followed her to the water.

Jere said, "You can get in the boats."

"What about you?"

"I will lead you." Then she looked at Josh and said, "Do not fear. I really *am* sent by Goel."

Something about her words and her manner must have satisfied Josh. He shoved the knife back in its sheath. "I guess we'll trust you. Come on, everybody, get in."

The Sleepers scrambled into the boats. Josh took one paddle and Dave the other. Then they looked back at Jere, who stood on the beach.

"Ready?" she asked.

"Ready," Josh said. "But what about you?"

Jere reached for a small object that dangled from her neck and blew it. It looked like some sort of horn. Then she pulled down over her face the plastic hood that had covered her hair. She touched a button on the complicated belt she wore. The transparent suit inflated.

At the same time, there was a loud splash.

Sarah whirled and was shocked to see a huge, round nose and a row of sharp teeth protrude from the water. At first, she thought it was a shark, but then she recognized the animal. "A porpoise," she cried out. "It's like Flipper."

Jere said, "Flipper? No, his name is Captain." She walked to the water, and the huge porpoise turned sideways. He wore a kind of saddle, and a simple bridle through his jaws. He croaked almost happily and moved so that Jere simply stepped into the saddle. She turned back to smile at them. "Follow me. I won't get too far ahead." Then she spoke to the porpoise. "Captain—on!" And the porpoise began to plow through the water.

The Sleepers stared after her as the boats followed.

"Well," Reb said, "I've been to two county fairs and three snake stompin's—but I ain't never seen nothing like that!"

Sarah leaned back and whispered to Josh, "I think she's all right."

Josh said solemnly, "She'd better be. Elmas isn't going to give up—or his Sanhedrin. Not till we're all dead." He looked after the beautiful young woman as the porpoise cut through the water. "If she is one of his spies, and if this is one of his traps, we're goners, Sarah."

But Sarah said, "No, she's not one of Elmas's people, I just know it."

* * *

The reputation of Elmas, Chief Interrogator of the Sanhedrin, was overwhelming. At the very mention of his name, people would tremble, and some prisoners had even been known to faint. But now, as he approached the throne room of the Tower, his own cruel face was filled with uncertainty. He wore a brilliant red robe with a heavy gold chain around his neck, bearing a strange medallion.

To himself he said, *I don't need to be afraid. I've always been faithful to Lord Necros.*

Still, when he was halted before the heavy door by two huge, armed guards, he noticed that his hands were trembling, and his knees felt so weak he was not sure he could stand.

One of the guards opened the door, disappeared, then was back, his heavy face staring down into the face of the Interrogator. "Lord Necros commands your presence."

Something about the words seemed filled with doom, but Elmas straightened up and forced down the fear that had been running through him. He followed the guard into a huge room.

A strange being sat on a throne. He was dressed in black, and a hood covered his face, but Elmas could see his powerful, clawlike hands, almost like eagles' talons. And in the shadow of the hood, the eyes of Lord Necros glowed red.

Here was something terrifying and evil, even to Elmas, who knew something about evil. This, he knew, was like nothing he himself could conjure up.

When Necros spoke, his voice was somehow full and yet had a deadened quality. It was as if a recording were speaking. Still, evil sounded in his speech.

"I have waited too long for your report."

Elmas's words ran over each other. "Yes . . . of course, my lord. But you must forgive me for . . . well, we have had difficulties—"

"Difficulties! I want results, not excuses. Give me your report."

For some time the Interrogator avoided the issue, and the red eyes of Lord Necros seemed to burn into his very soul.

Finally Necros said, "Enough. What is the result of your mission?"

"I . . . I regret to say that the . . . the Sleepers have . . . escaped."

As soon as the words were uttered, a searing pain began at the top of Elmas's head. With a groan, he grabbed his head and fell to the floor.

He sensed that Lord Necros was staring down at him as if he were some sort of insect. It seemed to Elmas that his head would fly off at any moment. "Please, my lord, I can explain—"

Lord Necros then gestured with one clawlike hand. At once the pain began to go away.

"Get to your feet," Lord Necros commanded. "Now I know what you are—a useless servant, indeed, of the Dark Lord."

"No!" Elmas cried out quickly. His hands were trembling so badly that he had to hold them together. Fear had driven almost everything from his mind. But he knew that he had only one chance. "I have a plan, my lord Necros."

"He has a plan." Necros raised his hand again, as if to send the pain flowing through Elmas again. Then he hesitated. "Well, what *is* this plan of yours? As I explained to you, we control most of the land now, so the Dark Lord commands that we control the sea. You have failed in that mission too, I suppose?"

"No, Lord Necros, please, just listen to me. The plan I have will gain us control of Atlantis—and it will mean the death of the Seven Sleepers."

Lord Necros leaned back on his throne, folded his hands together, and stared down at the Chief Interrogator. "And how are you going to perform these two miracles? You can't even catch seven children with all of your army!"

"But now we'll have them," Elmas said quickly. "You see, lord, it has been obvious from the first that we could never take Atlantis by force. Our people could not compete with the Atlantians under the sea by military power. Since we cannot, my lord, take the city by force, it must be taken from within."

"How do you propose to do that?"

For the first time, a trace of a smile and some assurance came to the face of the Interrogator. "One of the Atlantians has come over to our side."

"One of the enemy? Who is he?"

"Duke Lenomar."

Necros looked thoughtful, then demanded, "Is this true?"

"Yes, sire! He has gained the mind of Lord Aramis and clouded it so that the admiral obeys his commands."

"Then, as you say, the plan has possibilities. Now—"

Necros held out one claw again so that Elmas flinched, expecting the pain to strike him again. But it did not come. Instead, Lord Necros said, "Two things you will accomplish. First, the kingdom of Atlantis must be conquered. We must control the sea, and we can only control the sea when Atlantis is in our power."

"Yes, my lord, and the second thing?"

"As you have been told, the Sleepers must die. Somehow," he said, sounding puzzled, "these young people are tied up with the fate of the world. Our kingdom cannot tolerate their existence. They are the servants of Goel, therefore they must die."

"Yes, sire, I will see to it personally."

Lord Necros looked hard at him and said softly, "See that you do, Chief Interrogator. For if you do not, you will make a trip to one of my torturers, and if you think *your* questioners are harsh, you will think much more highly of ours."

Fear washed over Elmas. "My lord, it shall be done. Have I your leave to go and set the plan in motion?"

"Leave. And we will expect success, or you will meet a fate worse than death!"

3

A Step of Faith

Josh paddled as fast as he could in pursuit of the young woman Jere, who always kept herself well ahead.

"It looks like she's just gliding through the water," Sarah murmured. "I never saw anything like that. I know she's been sent by Goel, though."

Josh dug his paddle into the water. "Like I say, she'd better be. Because if we're going into a trap, I don't see any way out of it."

He put his strength into paddling and staying in the current. The river had broadened now, and although the ceiling was not quite so high, somehow he was not as frightened as before. The roar of the water had been the most terrifying of all.

For the next twenty minutes, they paddled. Finally Dave Cooper called back, "Look, I think there's light out there. See ahead of us?"

Sure enough, far ahead there seemed to be a pale flicker.

"Come on," Dave yelled, "I want to get out of this place."

Josh worked at keeping the boat in the middle of the stream. Dave was doing the same.

Then suddenly sunlight was filtering down, lighting the sides of the cave. And almost before Josh was ready, they shot out into the open, and the bright light blinded him.

Sarah put her hands over her eyes, crying out. Then she slowly removed them and looked around. "Why, look —we're at the ocean!"

Josh shaded his eyes. "It's some kind of a lagoon. But sure enough, that's ocean out there. Where's that girl?"

"Right over there," Sarah answered. "See, she's beckoning for us to come. Hurry, Josh. Let's get over to where she is."

Dave had seen the girl as well and turned his boat around. Soon both craft were drawn up on a white, sandy beach.

As the young people unloaded, Jake looked around, his brown eyes squinting against the bright sun. "You know, this looks like Hawaii. At least, it's got a beach like it. My folks took me there once."

Abigail pouted. "Well, we got out of that old cave anyway." She moved closer and held onto Dave's arm. "I wouldn't go back in that cave for anything in the world." She looked up at him with her beautiful eyes and fluttered her long lashes. "I think you did just wonderfully to get us out of there, Dave."

Standing a few feet away, Josh glared at Abigail and muttered under his breath, "I guess he had a little help." But when he caught Sarah's warning shake of the head, he stepped forward and said, "Well, Jere, is this the place?"

"Yes, it is." She waved her arm. "We're here and ready for the second part of the journey."

Josh looked out over the smooth sea, broken only at the shore by white water as the waves spilled over the shining sand. As far as he could see, there was nothing but water, water. He looked back at her. "You mean" — he swallowed hard— "we're going out there?"

Jere faced them all. She had pulled the plastic hood away from her face, and her raven-black curls blew in the soft, warm breeze. "Yes. That is, if you want to be obedient to Goel."

"How do you know Goel?" Sarah demanded.

Jere gave her a slight smile. "I have known him for a

long time, but we don't have time to talk about Goel just now. I must know if you're ready to go with me—out there." Once again she waved toward the vast, open reaches of the ocean.

Josh knew it was up to him, and he said, to forestall argument, "Yes, we made up our mind back in the cave. We voted on it, didn't we?" Some of the nods he got were not very strong, especially from Wash and Abigail, but Josh took it as approval. "All right, Jere. Where's the boat, if we're going to get out there? We can't swim."

With another smile, Jere reached down to her waist, took a tiny horn, and put it to her lips. She blew, and there was a high, shrill, keening noise, yet it had a melodious sound. When she lowered the horn, she said, "Just one moment."

Josh and the other Sleepers watched the sea, waiting for a boat to approach. Josh saw nothing.

After looking in all directions, Wash said, "Well, ma'am, I don't see nothing, and I'm telling you flat, I can't go out in that ocean without a—"

Suddenly the water seemed to boil a hundred yards down the beach. Josh stared in shock. "It's a whale!"

"A killer whale!" Dave whispered. "I saw one like him in a movie. That's what he is, a killer whale, all right. I never thought I'd see a real one."

Josh watched with amazement as the whale's rounded back and huge dorsal fin broke the surface again and again.

"And what's that thing he's pulling?" Reb called. "Look at that. It looks like a boat."

"It *is* a boat."

Jere had been watching their reaction with a smile. "That's what you'll be riding in."

The huge whale stopped twenty yards off shore. Josh could see clearly that some sort of harness was fastened to the front of the whale's body. The harness trailed back into a single cable, and to the cable was attached what looked like a large, flat sled. It looked very scarey.

"I can't ride in that thing!" Abbey moaned. "Oh, Dave, don't make me get in there!"

Dave Cooper always prided himself on not being afraid of anything, but now he swallowed quickly and shook his head, muttering. "Well, it does look a bit flimsy, doesn't it?"

A murmur went around the group.

Before there was a long argument, Sarah spoke up. "Look, we voted back in the cave, and it ought to be obvious we didn't have a hope in the world of getting away from the Sanhedrin and the soldiers. But the stone wall opened, and we made our way through the river, and Jere came to lead us out. And now there's a boat."

"You're right." Josh nodded. "Come on, let's get in that thing." He managed a grin. "I think they used to call it a Nantucket Sleigh Ride back in the whaling days. They harpooned a whale, and the whale would pull their little boat all over the ocean. Well, let's just pretend this is a sleigh ride."

"That is a good thought, Joshua," Jere said. "Come, you and I will bring in the boat for the others."

Josh felt much less brave than he seemed, wading out into the water with Jere toward the strange craft. Together they pulled the boat to shore. It was made of some lightweight but very strong material. There were several seats and several compartments, obviously watertight, and Josh began to grow interested.

"Come on," he said. "After all, it's just a boat." When everyone hesitated, he said, "Come on, how many kids get a chance to ride behind a real killer whale?"

Dave, obviously embarrassed by his own uncertainty, said, "Sure. Come on, Abbey. It's just another boat ride." He splashed out, holding Abigail's hand, and the two of them clambered aboard.

Wash, Reb, and Jake followed. Sarah came last, and Josh helped her into the front seat.

Jere said, "Not many young people would have the courage to do what you're doing. I believe that Goel has sent me to the right place at the right time. Now we must go."

She blew her whistle, and the porpoise was at her side, sticking his head up, grinning at her, it seemed. Slipping into the saddle, Jere said, "On, Captain, on!" and, holding the reins in one hand, she threw her other hand forward.

The huge porpoise began to plunge through the sea, and then the great whale stirred forward, not as actively as the porpoise, but magnificently. He stayed very close to the surface.

"Look," Josh said. "You can see his tail."

"Why, it's on sideways, ain't it?" Reb said. "Not like a real fish."

"That's one of the differences between whales and fish," Josh said. "They have horizontal tails, and that's the way they get their power. They breathe air too—instead of having gills."

"I never knew that," Reb muttered.

Suddenly the whale gave a lunge, and the sled seemed to fly over the water. Reb pulled his hat off and let out a wild cowboy yell. "*Whoo—ooo!*" he bellowed. "Ride 'em, cowboy!"

All the passengers in the sea sled gripped the handholds tightly. Most seemed afraid at first, yet there was something wonderful about the giant whale as he knifed his way beneath the waves, rising and falling, the huge tail propelling him forward. The sled flew after him, bobbing up and down as the whale slowed or sped up, and always there was Jere out in front, as Captain plunged ahead.

"That looks like fun, don't it?" Reb said to Sarah. "I'd kind of like to ride a critter like that. The only thing I ever rode is horses, four-footed stuff. But that looks like a fun critter to ride."

For a long time the sleigh slid across the water, leaving behind it a white wake that broke the greenness of the ocean. The water was smooth. The only sound was Jere's occasional cry, encouraging them to come on, and once in a while the mighty tail of the killer whale rose out of the water completely and slapped the surface with a resounding crash.

"Wow, that's some flyswatter he's got, isn't it, now?" Wash said with admiration. His eyes were large, but seemingly he had overcome his fear to some extent. "I sure hope we get to land pretty soon, though. Ain't much I dislike more than water, and I never seen so much water in all my days."

Five minutes later, Jere suddenly guided the porpoise around, the whale stopped, and the sled glided smoothly to a halt. Jere urged the porpoise closer, slipped on board, and smiled at the Sleepers.

"Did you enjoy your ride?"

When they all nodded, she sobered and said, "The next part will require a little more courage, I'm afraid."

Josh looked about at the endless water, and Sarah said, "But I thought we were going to your home, Jere. I don't see anything but water."

Jere was silent for a moment. She seemed trying to think of some way to break bad news to them, and they all grew very quiet.

"What is it, Jere?" Josh demanded. "Is something wrong?"

"I'm afraid you'll think so." She bit her lip just like an ordinary girl, and Josh saw again how very pretty she was. "My home is here."

When they had all looked around, almost wildly, Dave said, "Here? There's nothing here but water."

"Not here on top." Jere leaned over and pointed down. "My home is in Atlantis, which is twenty fathoms beneath where we are right now."

Everyone looked down, but there was nothing to see except blue-green water.

"Twenty fathoms down!" Dave exclaimed. "Why . . ." He couldn't finish his sentence.

Josh swallowed. "Is that true, Jere? I've heard of the lost city of Atlantis all my life, but I thought it was just a fairy tale."

"It may have been, years ago, but my people fled the land after the Burning." She meant after the war, Josh knew. "Living was too terrible on the earth, so we discovered this city, and we have learned to live down there."

"How can you live under the ocean?" Abigail whispered, her eyes wide. "I don't even like to think about it."

Jere said, "I cannot explain it to you, but this is the moment when you must decide. My home is down there." She pointed again to the depths. Then she raised her voice and threw her head back, her hair flying in the breeze. "And Goel has sent me to bring you to Atlantis. I think that you might save our people. Will you come?"

Josh was sure that not a person who heard her voice had any desire at all to go to the city of Atlantis. His friends looked at each other with frightened expressions. Unless something was said, he knew, the whole idea of the Seven Sleepers would be lost. So he took a deep breath. "I don't believe that we were brought out here to quit. I believe we're here for a purpose and that somehow we're going to do great good."

"But Josh," Sarah whispered, "twenty fathoms down, and most of us can't even swim."

Jere said quickly, "You will not have to swim. If you

29

will but trust me one more time, I will take you to my home, and you will be as safe there as you are in this boat."

Josh stared at her, and so did all the others.

The silence was thick enough to cut with a knife, and finally it was the smallest and youngest member, Wash, aged twelve, who spoke. "Miss Jere, I'll go with you. I believe you wouldn't hurt us."

That saved the day for the Sleepers, for if Wash, small and young and deathly afraid of water as he was, would agree, how could the rest refuse?

Josh said at once, "It's settled, then. We'll go." He turned to Jere. "How do we get down there?"

Instead of answering, Jere opened a locker on the side of the sled. She pulled out a small package and handed it to Josh. "I have one of these for each of you." She touched her own plastic-looking uniform. "This diving suit, as you might call it, will protect you. Put them on at once."

"Over our clothes?" Abigail demanded.

"No, they are swimsuits that fit all sizes. One for men and one for women. If you girls will go to the front of the boat, the young men will turn the other way while you change. Then you'll do the same for them."

And that was the way it went. When Sarah opened her package she found a sea-green one-piece bathing suit, much like the one she had worn to the beach. But this suit was both flexible and hard and seemed to be made of overlapping green scales. Quickly she slipped into it, and Jere said, "Now, put on your diving suits."

Sarah stepped into the plastic uniform, pulled it up, and found that it closed around her neck tightly. She pulled out the belt and was surprised to find how heavy it was.

When all had on their swimsuits and uniforms, they gathered about Jere.

30

"The belt is your life-support system," she said. "It is what will let you live under the sea. It contains compressed air in three of these pockets. It has a tiny radio, so that you will be able to communicate, even under water, not only with those close to you, but even with those who're far off."

Then Jere taught them how to attach the tubes and wires. "Slip the hood over your head, and you'll find it will tighten with this fastening."

The young people awkwardly did as she told them.

As soon as she had hers on, Sarah had a moment's fright. "I'm going to smother," she cried out.

"No, simply turn that button on the front of your belt."

Sarah did so, and immediately a gust of fresh oxygen poured into her suit. It inflated the suit slightly, and she was amazed to find that now she could not feel the warm wind.

"It's insulated so you won't feel the cold of the ocean," Jere said. "You can all breathe?" She inspected their air hoses and then stood back. "Now, you must not be afraid. I know this is a new world for you, but Goel never fails." Then she reached down, took out the small horn, put it to her lips, and blew again.

For what seemed a long while, there was nothing, and then suddenly the ocean boiled.

"It's porpoises! With the same kind of harnesses that Captain has," Josh called out.

Sarah asked, "Are we supposed to ride these?"

"Yes, they will take you down to the city," Jere said. "All you have to do is get on and hang on. You can breathe, you can shut your eyes if you want to, and when you open them you'll be safe in Atlantis. Come."

The young people scrambled to the side of the boat. One by one Jere called the great porpoises forward and assigned a porpoise to each Sleeper.

Sarah stepped out of the boat and settled awkwardly into the saddle. She was delighted by the sleek touch of the porpoise and how well she seemed to fit. There was a harness that he held between his teeth, and she gripped it tightly. She did call over, "Reb, you ought to be better than any of us at this, since you're a rider."

Reb grinned at her, his white teeth flashing in the sun. "Well, I hope so. But I never rode a critter like this without no feet."

Then Jere said, "Remember, you must hang on. Do not turn loose. Remember to breathe—don't try to hold your breath. In the name of Goel, we go to Atlantis!"

4

The Lost City of Atlantis

For Sarah, the sudden plunge under the surface of the sea was one of the most frightening experiences of her life. She had never swum in anything except a swimming pool, and now as the porpoise twisted and her arms were pulled by the bridle, fear ran through her. The only shock of coldness, however, was on her hands, the one part of her body that was left uncovered. She was grateful for the warm diving suit, but this was probably her only consolation.

Quickly she looked around and realized, to her surprise, that she could see almost as well under the water as above. The plastic that covered her head served as a diving mask. She saw the lovely blue-green water lit by the sunshine above, and for one moment she forgot her fear.

Josh was close on her right, hanging onto his reins with both hands. He gave her a sudden glance. She saw his lips move and was delighted to hear his voice. It came through a tiny radio that was built into the diving suit.

He smiled brightly. "Hang on, Sarah, we're going to make it fine."

Apparently all the others heard him too—the radio seemed to transmit to all the Sleepers. Sarah noticed that Wash and Reb, who had become friends after a rough beginning, were sticking close together. Reb looked as if he were enjoying the ride, but Wash was hanging on grimly, his eyes shut tight.

"Watch Wash carefully," Josh ordered. "Don't let him fall off."

The others seemed to be doing well. Dave was side by side with Abbey, reaching out to her from time to time and murmuring encouragement.

They descended deeper and deeper, and Sarah was startled to see more fish than she'd ever seen in her life. A swarm of brightly colored scarlet fish, thousands and thousands of them, passed below, almost turning the water crimson with their fiery color. Then, as if at a signal, they all turned at once and made their way off through the green water.

I wonder how they all know to turn at the same time? Sarah thought.

Down, down, down they went. Several times she saw strange spectacles. One rather frightening sight was a school of barracuda. They hung suspended in the water, their lower jaws unhinged, and there was a cold hunger in their eyes.

"Don't worry," Jere said. "They won't attack. You're all doing fine. And it isn't far now."

The water became somewhat darker, but still visibility was good.

Suddenly Jere said, "There it is. That's my home, Atlantis."

Below them was a display that Sarah would never forget—the lost city of Atlantis. She almost forgot to breathe and then, remembering Jere's warning, took several gulps of air. *Why, it's beautiful,* she thought.

The city had high towers and turrets much like a castle, except that it was built of a strange material, somewhat like the coral she had seen. It reared itself up from the depths of the sea and glowed with a faint light. Here and there what appeared to be bright-colored stones dotted the walls of the towers and parapets. She could also see small, thick windows. She could not see inside, but there seemed to be light.

"Careful now," Jere cautioned. "We're going into an air lock. Just follow me very closely. The porpoises know how."

Sarah watched as Jere slowed the pace of Captain and approached what seemed to be a round dome on the ocean floor. There was a passageway, six or seven feet wide and at least eight feet tall, and the water seemed to flow in and out of it.

Jere drew up her porpoise by the door and turned to smile at them. Waving at the entrance, she said, "All inside now."

Sarah was the first to enter. She passed through the portal of the bubble, and for a moment all was dark. Then a brilliant light shone. Suddenly her head broke water, and she gasped with relief. She found herself in a large domed room. The ceiling glowed with some sort of light she didn't understand.

One by one the other Sleepers popped up around her, and finally Jere herself entered. She raised her head above water and sat there looking at them. "I congratulate you Sleepers," she said with a smile. "You've done well. You can remove your hoods now." As she removed her own and watched as the others did the same, she seemed amused at their relief.

Josh took a deep breath. "Why, that's fresh air. How can that be down here, Jere?"

Jere slipped off her porpoise, for the water was only waist deep. "It's supplied by pumps that bring the air down from above. Come now, we must go to the palace."

Taking deep breaths, Sarah thought the fresh air seemed as sweet as anything she had ever taken into her lungs.

Jere moved out of the water and stepped up onto a small platform. "This way."

She approached a door, which opened without her even touching it, and the Sleepers crowded close behind her. They entered a long corridor where the ceiling and walls glowed with the same kind of light that had lit the pressure chamber.

Jere said, "Quickly now." She hurried along the passage until she came to a large door. She spoke a word that Sarah did not understand, and the door, which seemed made of stone, swung slowly open. Jere said, "This way," and stepped inside.

Sarah saw that they were now in a very large room indeed—obviously some kind of meeting room, for there were long tables and chairs, carved with fantastic designs. And suddenly Sarah knew what it looked like. "It looks like a dining room in a large castle," she said aloud.

"Why, that's right," Dave said. "I've seen them on TV and in books." He turned to Jere. "Is this some kind of banquet room?"

"Sometimes it's used for that. It's also a place where we meet to take votes on different matters."

"You must be a democracy then," Jake said with interest, his blue eyes glowing. "Do you have a president?"

"President? Democracy?" Jere shook her head. "I don't know about any of those. We have a king and a queen, but still the people may say what they wish, and the king will listen. Come now."

But before she could move, Reb made a discovery. "Look," he cried out, running over to the wall. "There are windows. You can see out."

The Sleepers crowded around what seemed to be portholes, which looked directly out into the sea.

"Why, it's like being inside an aquarium. Look at that!" Reb shouted. "A shark!"

A huge tiger shark rolled by, his old eyes seeming to glance toward them, and then he moved on silently.

Josh asked, "How can all this be? What keeps the water out, Jere?"

36

"This city was once above the ocean floor—at least we think so. On an island," she answered. "But it sank beneath the sea, as islands sometimes do. My people came many, many years ago. We began to seal the buildings. It was a slow process, but we discovered how to compress the air and how to make the joints tight. So now what we're living in is really a sealed city."

"A city under the sea," Abbey said with a smile. "You know that's rather nice. I think it's romantic. Don't you, Dave?"

Dave frowned. "Well, I don't know about romantic, but it sure is impressive."

Josh said, "Look at that! What's that out there?"

"Those are the guards of our city—our navy," Jere said quietly.

Sarah moved closer. She saw sharks—killer sharks, she thought. They were coming in ranks like soldiers, and mounted on each shark was a man wearing a plastic diving suit and cradling in his arms some sort of weapon. It looked like a powerful spear gun but with a larger base than she had ever seen.

"That's the second battalion of our navy, led by Lord Daveon," Jere said. "You have come to Atlantis at a bad time—a time of war." She blinked. "But no more of this. I know you're all tired. I'll show you to your chambers."

"What will we do next, Jere?" Josh asked.

Jere smiled, looking lovely in the light that came from the ceiling. "For a while, we will rest. Then later we will meet with the king and queen, and you will find out more. I'll show you your rooms."

* * *

The Sleepers, despite themselves, their excitement, and the tense situation, did rest.

Sarah was awakened some time later by a knock. She

opened the door of the room she shared with Abbey and saw a tall, handsome young man of sixteen or seventeen years, with dark hair and dark eyes. He wore a sea-green uniform having a gold dolphin over his breast. "My name is Valar. I have come to escort you ladies to the king's table."

Sarah stared, for she had never seen such a handsome young man in all of her life.

He was fully six feet tall and strong, in spite of his obvious youth. He stood smiling down at her as Abbey joined them. "May I know your names?" he asked.

"I'm Sarah, and this is Abbey." Abbey too, she was aware, was filled with wonder at the regal bearing of the young man, but not so awestruck that she could not smile—which caused her dimples to appear. This, Sarah also knew, was a fact of which Abbey was well aware, and she did it when she wanted to attract attention. "We're ready, I suppose. But we don't have anything to wear to a royal banquet."

"Later on, you will be provided with suitable clothes. But for now, His Majesty and the queen will understand."

He led them down several corridors and finally stopped before a large door where two guards stood posted with powerful looking spear guns in their hands. They stepped aside, opened the doors, and Valar waved a hand saying, "You may enter now."

The two young women went in and discovered that the boys were already there.

"Over here," Valar said. "You can all sit together." And taking the arm of each young lady, he led them to a place at the long table. He saw them seated, then stepped back.

Across the room Sarah saw a man and woman sitting on a raised platform—obviously the king and queen of Atlantis—and beside them, to the king's right, sat Jere!

Jere saw their surprise and said, "Now that we're all here, let me introduce you. Your Majesties, I present to you the Seven Sleepers." She called off their names and then said, "I would like for you to meet my parents, King Cosmos and Queen Mab."

The news that Jere was the princess of the kingdom of Atlantis took Sarah off guard. She saw the other Sleepers stare in surprise too.

Jere nodded, saying, "It has been my great pleasure to bring you to my father's kingdom. Your Majesty, would you greet our guests?"

King Cosmos was a big man with pale skin, a long white beard, and wise old eyes. He wore a sea-green robe, also with a dolphin over the breast, and on his head was a crown. Queen Mab was obviously younger. Her dark hair was graying, but she had fine eyes, and she smiled at them.

King Cosmos said, "You are welcome to our kingdom. We were concerned about you."

Queen Mab had a more gentle voice. She said, "We will eat now, and then later we will talk."

The Sleepers never forgot that meal. Most of the food, they were told, was taken from the sea. The salad was made from seaweed that tasted as delicious as anything Sarah had ever eaten. There was a soup made from turtle, and steaks from red snapper. There were even desserts at the end of the meal. She couldn't imagine where they had come from.

When the meal was over, King Cosmos nodded at them and said, "It would please us to hear your histories."

All the group looked at Joshua, who stood to his feet. "Your Majesty, I am not sure exactly what you mean."

"Our daughter has told us somewhat of your story, but we must know more, for we are in a time of trouble here in Atlantis. Begin at the beginning, if you will."

So Josh began back at the time when he was on the old earth, which seemed long, long ago. He told how the Sleepers had been put in time capsules, how he had been awakened first, and then how he'd found the others, who were scattered over the earth. Finally he related how he had to fight the armies of the Sanhedrin, and especially Elmas, the Chief Interrogator.

Josh ended by saying, "We barely escaped death before we found the underground river. But we have been led, I'm bound to say, Your Majesty, by Goel."

At the name of Goel, the king and queen both smiled.

Queen Mab said, "I am glad that you have been in such capable hands."

King Cosmos said, "Yes, when the Princess Jere told us of her vision and how she had been instructed by Goel to find you, I was not certain about it. But now we are glad that you have been brought to us."

"Father," Jere said, "perhaps it might be well if you explained what is happening in our kingdom."

"Of course." A gloomy look crossed the king's face. "As you know, the dark powers of Elmas, and others even worse, are striving to overcome the earth. There is a house that is rising called the House of Goel. Do you know of this?"

"Yes, sire," Josh said instantly. "We know of it and of the legends that concern the Seven Sleepers and that at one time the House of Goel will be filled."

"Very true, very true," King Cosmos said, "but we have had a revolution here in our kingdom of Atlantis."

"A revolution?" Josh asked.

"Yes."

The king and queen both looked downcast, and Jere was so disturbed that she rose and walked away to look out a porthole.

Sarah's sharp eyes saw this and knew there was

more to come. "What sort of revolution, Your Majesty?" she asked.

"Enough for now to say that we are under siege and that one very close and dear to us has led our kingdom into rebellion. But tomorrow you will meet with the elders of Atlantis, and then you will know all. Now I assign to our nephew Valar the keeping of all of you. Valar," he said, "see that our guests are well-treated and bring them to the meeting of the elders in the morning."

The king rose with the queen and walked out of the room. All the Sleepers stood and bowed as they passed by. As soon as they were gone, Valar said, "Well, I am your host, it seems, and I will do my best to make you feel at home." He moved to put his hands on the arms of Sarah and Abbey. "If you will come this way, I will show you around the castle."

"He sure knows how to make a move on the ladies, don't he now?" Reb grinned. "He made straight for those girls like a hog for slop."

Despite his flash of jealousy, Josh had to grin at the way Reb put it. "Well, he's got good taste—you can say that much for him. Come on now, I don't want to miss any of this."

5

Council of War

J osh, I can't believe you talked to me like that!"
Sarah glared.

Josh had come to her room and, finding her alone,
had immediately said, "Sarah, I'm ashamed of the way
you're behaving." He knew there was anger and disap-
pointment in his face.

"Behaving about what?"

"About that Valar fellow."

And it was clear all at once that Sarah thought Josh
was jealous. She had snapped back angrily, and now she
stared at him, her face rather pale.

Josh calmed himself. "Look, Sarah, you know we've
been good friends, not just here but in Oldworld. You and
I have been together longer than any of the others, and I
hate to see you making such a spectacle out of yourself."

"Spectacle? Is that what you call it?" Her mouth grew
tight, and she drew her shoulders up. "I would call it behaving politely." And then she added spitefully, "Something I think you might study, Joshua Adams."

"Politely? That's a hot one," Josh shot back. He
shook his head angrily. "You're no better than Abbey.
You've always been critical of her because she hung on
Dave and me, and now you're doing the very same thing
with this fellow."

"Jealous, that's what you are. Jealous," Sarah lashed
out. "And as for hanging onto you, as you call it, I don't
think you'll have to worry about that anymore."

"Fine with me!" Josh's voice trembled slightly, for,

although he was angry with Sarah, he had a very special feeling for her. Now he realized that he had handled things awkwardly and said to himself, *Why can't I ever do anything right? I should have gotten Dave or Reb or somebody else to talk to her. Now she'll hate me forever!*

He hoped he let none of this show in his face and turned to go. Just as he reached the door, there was a knock. He opened it.

And there stood Valar. "Oh, hello, Joshua. I've come to escort all of you to the Council meeting."

"I'm glad you came for all of us," Josh said pointedly. "I'll call the others, and you can take all of us to the Council meeting right away."

Sarah glared again. Stepping forward she took Valar's arm and smiled up at him. "I'm ready, Valar."

"Well, come along, then," he said. "You bring the others, Josh."

"All right," Josh snapped and quickly moved down the hall knocking on the other doors.

When they were all in the hall, Dave looked down the passageway and saw Valar and Sarah walking along, engaged in deep conversation. "Well—" he grinned "—I guess we know who's important around here. At least to Valar."

"He came down to show *all of us* to the council," Josh growled, "but I guess we'll have to get there the best way we can."

They followed Valar and Sarah along the corridor, which made several turns, and passed through several large rooms. Finally, they came to a door.

Valar said, "They are expecting you."

Sarah smiled. "Thank you, Valar."

"Why, you're welcome, Sarah. Now, I think you'd better go in."

When they entered, Sarah looked around quickly. Aware that Josh was furious with her, she did not meet his eyes. The room, she saw, was not particularly large. There was a table shaped like a half moon, and around the outer edge sat six men dressed in green robes. All wore the sign of the dolphin on medallions around their necks. Across from them, ten feet away on a low dais, King Cosmos sat, Queen Mab to his right and Princess Jere to his left.

The king said at once, "I wanted my brethren to ask these young people to our Council, for it is clear that somehow they are tied in with the destiny of our poor country. They are the servants of Goel."

He waved to the right, and the Seven Sleepers moved in the direction of the gesture, where seven chairs waited for them. Valar moved with them and took his stance behind Sarah, watching the proceedings.

Sarah looked up at him, thinking of what he had told her. She was not sure the others knew that Valar was the son of the king's only brother. She thought suddenly, *It seems to me—if things work here like they do in some countries—some day Valar might be king of Atlantis.*

But she had no time to think further about that for King Cosmos said, "I have called this council because our country is in a critical hour. I ask you, Womar, Chief of the Council, to speak to these young people and then to all of us concerning the situation."

A tall man, strong but pale and past his first youth, rose. He had a closely trimmed beard, shot through with silver, piercing black eyes, and a mouth like a steel trap. There was a sternness in him that one saw in men from time to time, but not cruelty.

Sarah overheard Josh murmur to Dave, "Not a man I'd like to cross."

Dave nodded, and the two of them began to listen carefully.

"For generations," Womar said, "our nation has been ruled by monarchs and by the Council of Elders. Throughout all of our history, we have had one goal—to keep our honor bright." He frowned suddenly and let his words fall slowly. "Those who are dishonorable are given the choice of leaving—or death."

He turned his head suddenly and, Sarah thought, somehow seemed to look directly into the eyes of each Sleeper. "It is highly painful for me to speak of this matter. For many months we have been aware that the Dark Power desires to rule our kingdom under the sea. He wants to control the ocean, but he cannot unless he controls Atlantis. He tried force, but we easily drove the servants of the Dark Lord away."

He paused, and there was a hollow silence. Sarah watched intently the workings of his face. Then Womar shook his head sadly and lowered his voice. "We were betrayed by one trusted by us all."

A breeze seemed to sway the Council. Glancing upward, Sarah saw that the king and the queen—and especially Jere—were disturbed.

"The Lord High Admiral Aramis, the favorite of the elders—and of the royal family—fell under the sway of the Dark Lord. He was the best of us all, the brightest star in our sky. But he led a revolt against the crown, and now, at any moment, we look for him to come with his powerful navy to storm Atlantis."

One of the elders, a tall, thin man, asked, "Have our scouts reported anything new, Chief Elder Womar?"

"Only that Aramis has built for himself a mighty

structure—or rather I should say he has taken over that which King Cosmos built."

Cosmos stared at him. "You mean he has taken the Citadel of Neptune?"

"I fear so, Your Majesty. I grieve to make this report, for I know that this is not pleasant for you to hear."

The king looked toward the Seven Sleepers and said slowly, "The Citadel of Neptune has been the dream of my heart. I love Atlantis, but it grows crowded, and we need more room for our people. So it has been my delight to build a new city, a more modern one, that will house many of our people. It is the finest thing that we in Atlantis have ever built."

He went on to describe the Citadel of Neptune, which sounded very modern to Sarah. *It sounds like something out of a comic strip—a city built under the sea. But after seeing this place, I don't doubt anything.*

Womar continued. "He has established a powerful base at the Citadel and is even now, our scouts have told us, training a huge navy." He shrugged. "Well, perhaps not huge, but well-trained."

As Womar spoke of Aramis, Sarah noticed that Jere had become highly upset. Her face grew tense, and finally she dropped her head and stared at the floor.

Womar said, "I have asked Lord Deneor, our War Admiral, to speak."

Lord Deneor was an elderly man indeed. He was not tall and did not appear strong, and he certainly was past his prime. Of all the elders, he was not the man Sarah would have chosen to be War Admiral, for he was past the days of leading men into battle.

Elder Lord Deneor stood and began to speak, his voice clear but not strong. "Your Majesties, and my fellow elders of the Council, none here grieves more than I at the revolt of the Lord High Admiral, as he was once called—Aramis. We all loved him and trusted him."

He lowered his eyes and seemed unable to speak for a moment. "I poured into him all the lore that I have learned over many years—from all of the battles that have taken place in the past. All of the strategy, all of the wisdom, such as I had, I poured into his young mind. And it had been my joy to see him one day take his place as Lord High Admiral." Here he glanced at the royalty, hesitated, and said, "Or even higher, perhaps."

Sarah noticed that, at this last statement, Jere suddenly turned her head away and stared out the window, so that none could see her face.

Deneor went on to speak for several minutes about his loss of Aramis. Sarah found herself curious about this man who had risen so high and yet had led a revolt against the very people who seemed to love him the most.

The king suddenly asked point blank, "Lord Deneor, I ask you, can the kingdom survive? Can we hold off the forces of Aramis?"

Lord Deneor lifted his head, and tears glistened in his eyes. "Your Majesty, I must in all honesty tell you that the only way we can survive is if some kind of miracle takes place."

A hush came over the room, and Deneor let it run on for several moments. Then he said, "I must tell you this, for I would not raise false hopes. Many of our best sailors have joined in the revolt with Aramis. He is a mariner beyond compare, as you all know. Brave beyond any of the men that followed him, strong, and above all a strategist and a sailor of utmost ability. When he leads his navy here against us, we will do our best, but we are weak, and he is strong."

For almost an hour the talk went back and forth across the table, as the Sleepers listened, saying nothing.

It was obvious that Aramis, who had been the Lord High Admiral, was high in the favor of the king and queen—and Jere as well, Sarah saw. He had been the pride of the royal kingdom, and somehow he had fallen.

Lord Deneor explained his plans for defending the kingdom, and they sounded weak, even to Sarah.

Finally, Womar rose again. "Let us hear from the Sleepers."

At first, none of the Sleepers responded, and then Dave dug his elbow into Josh's ribs. "Get up, Josh. It's up to you."

* * *

Feeling very weak, Joshua Adams stood before the elders of Atlantis, the king, the queen, and the princess. He had no idea what to say and finally began by confessing, "Of all those qualified to speak, surely I would be the last. We are all mere youths. We have been brought to this world from an older world that is now gone. All we know is that we are the servants of Goel, and we have been told, according to many legends and many old songs, that when the Seven Sleepers awake, the House of Goel will be filled."

"Yes, yes," Womar said. "We have all heard the songs. That is why we have brought you here—or rather, shall I say, Goel has brought you here. Can you tell us, have you any idea of how we can meet this critical hour?"

Josh hesitated, then asked, "Before I answer, may I ask one question?"

"Of course," the king said at once. "What is it, my boy?"

"Well, from all I hear, Aramis was a man of great ability, and no man could have gained the confidence of the elders and of Your Majesties unless he had good qualities." He paused again. "How could such a man revolt against his king and his country?"

Queen Mab answered, "Only through the powers of the Dark Lord could such a thing happen. We do not know what came to pass—all we know is that something happened to Aramis. He is no longer the child or the young man or the strong warrior that we knew and loved. He has become our enemy, and it can only be because the Dark Lord has in some way used his forces to cloud the mind of our former admiral."

Joshua nodded, understanding. "We have seen what Elmas, the Chief Interrogator, can do with minds. As a matter of fact, he has used his power on us. Now as to your question, I must say, Your Majesty, and to the council, we have no notion of why we have been brought here."

Silence fell, and everyone looked glum. Then Joshua raised his voice. "But Goel has never failed. He has used the men and beasts of Nuworld to save us. And I, for one, believe that he has saved us for a purpose. So I say to the Council and to you, Your Majesties, that the Seven Sleepers are here, and now there is no choice but to wait for Goel to speak."

The king slammed his fist on the arm of his throne. "Well spoken, young man." His face appeared noble and his eyes clear as he looked at the Sleepers. "We will hold our honor dear—and wait for Goel to speak."

6
Sarah's Visitor

The next day, very early, all seven young people were awakened at what seemed an inordinately early hour. Valar herded them down the corridor to the mess hall, where they were seated at a long table.

At once, servants brought in food, and Valar sat down across from Sarah with a grin. "I would advise you to eat heartily. You have a hard day in front of you."

"A hard day?" Josh demanded, glaring. "What sort of day are you talking about?"

"Why, the Council and His Royal Majesty have commanded that you be trained in the skills and arts of Atlantis."

"We've done fine by ourselves so far," Josh snapped. He looked at the plate that had been put in front of him. The food smelled delicious, but he said churlishly, "I never eat much breakfast, and I think we've done fine alone!"

Valar stared at Josh. A smile played around his lips, and he winked at Sarah. "Yes, I'm sure you have. Sarah's told me about some of your adventures, but you will have to admit that our country is different from anything you have ever known. I understand that some of you cannot even swim." There was wonder in his voice. "We'll remedy that first."

Wash had been stuffing food into his mouth, but at these words he looked up and said, "But Mr. Valar, I can't swim a lick. Never could. And I'm afraid of water."

Valar laughed, his white teeth flashing, and he looked very sure of himself. "Don't worry about that. I'm a good teacher. All of you will learn to swim. It's not like it is on the surface, I assure you. And there will be some other things that will be—oh, a little more difficult."

The Sleepers did eat heartily—though some of the items were not even recognizable—and for the next hour, while they waited for breakfast to settle, Valar gave them a tour of the defenses of the city.

As they walked along the parapets, he waved at the windows. "Now these are all sealed, of course. There are only four entrances into the castle itself, and these are heavily guarded. But if the enemy throws all of his force against them . . ." He shrugged, and doubt came into his eyes. "I'm not sure that we will be able to hold out."

He led them down to a room that had an air lock and fitted them out again with the clear plastic diving suits that they had worn before.

"You've already become accustomed to these. But before, you were doing nothing but riding. This time you'll be doing the swimming." He glanced over at Wash and at Abbey, who looked very frightened, and said, "Don't worry. We'll have plenty of help. There's nothing that can happen to you."

Valar assisted them in adjusting their suits and explained how the compressed air worked. If one chamber failed, there were four others, and they had plenty of air for more than eight hours outside the city itself.

"Besides," he said, "you won't feel the pressure of the water because the oxygen inside pumps up your suit. You won't even know you're deep down under the ocean." He explained again the use of the radios. "All right, we're ready to try it. Now this is what makes all the difference." He reached into the equipment box and pulled out a pair of flippers. "You've all seen these, I suppose?"

"Yes, I have," Dave said. "I went snorkeling once off the coast of Belize, in the reefs. That's what we used, all right."

"I don't know about Belize, but you can certainly use them in Atlantis." Valar looked at Wash, picked up a pair of the smaller flippers, and said, "Put these on, young fellow, and I'll show you how simple it is. Suppose we let you go first while the others watch."

Valar—Josh was sure—had picked the weakest member of the team, knowing that if he could teach Wash, then they all could learn.

Wash slipped on the huge black fins and looked down at them. "I look like a frog."

Valar laughed. "Well, you'll be about as awkward as a frog on dry land. These things are hard to walk with. Come on, and I'll give you a lesson." He reached down and assisted Wash to his feet, and Wash stumbled across the room towards the water in the exchange tank.

"Now," Valar said, as Wash stood up to his waist in water, "I'll come with you, and the rest of you can watch through the ports. You see, Wash," he said, "you don't even use your arms to swim. All you do is kick your feet, and you'll be surprised how you go right along, just like a fish. Don't be afraid."

Wash did look afraid, but there was determination in his bright eyes too. "I'll try. If I get drowned," he said with a faint grin, "I don't guess I can drown but once."

Valar laughed again. "You won't drown. Just kick your feet. To turn right, kick your left foot. To turn left, kick your right foot. Come along, now." He fastened their helmets, led the small black boy farther into the tank, and they both ducked under.

As Josh looked through the window, he saw at once that Valar was staying right beside Wash.

"Look," Reb yelled out. "He's got it already! He's swimming like a fish!"

And sure enough, Wash was. For the next fifteen minutes, Valar led him through various maneuvers. Once he brought him up to the porthole, so that Wash could look inside and see his friends smiling out at him. He grinned broadly and motioned for them to come on out and join him.

Soon Valar had led them all out of the air tank, and they were swimming along smoothly underwater. Sarah said later that she knew fear for a moment as the green water closed about her, but in five minutes she found that it was the most delightful experience of her life. She had no trouble at all breathing, and the water was so clear she could see for many feet. As for movement, it was the easiest thing she had ever done. She clamped her hands to her side as Valar taught her, kicked her feet, and went along as smoothly as any fish.

For the next hour, they trained themselves on how to make turns, how to go up, and how to go down. Finally, Valar said, "All right, that's enough for one session. We'll go out again later."

When they were inside, Reb said, "Shoot, that was more fun than riding a bronco. I wish I'd of knowed all this time I was a good swimmer. I'd of had more fun at it."

Valar smiled. "You'll be a little sore after a while. You're using some muscles you don't ordinarily use, but you'll grow strong quickly."

This proved to be the case. They were all sore the next morning, but by the time they had trained four days, they had worked the soreness out, and all had become adept at the rudiments of swimming.

Valar was pleased and said so. "You've done very well. Now we get down to more serious matters."

He led them to a room that was lined with lockers. In each was one of the strange-looking spear guns that Josh had seen the mariner guards carry.

"This is what you'll use as your primary weapon," Valar said. He pulled down one gun and a quiver of ar-

54

rows. Basically, the gun looked much like a rifle, except that it was made of some very lightweight metal.

"Really, it's very simple. You put your spear in like this—" Valar demonstrated carefully, sliding a spear with a three-foot shaft into the chamber made for it "—then you put your weapon off safety." He raised the spear gun and aimed it at a wooden, rounded figure down the hall. "Then you pull the trigger."

Zing. There was a hiss of air, and when Josh looked, he saw the spear quivering in the wood figure.

"If that had been an enemy, he'd be dead," Valar said in an offhand fashion. "We'll practice in here, loading and unloading. That really is the hardest part. Actually, all you do is point your spear gun at the enemy and pull the trigger."

For the next two days, they trained as hard as they could, learning the use of the spear guns. Josh discovered that there were different types of spears and that the best mariners carried some of each. There was the armor-piercing spear, which had a tough tip on it, very sharp and keen enough to pierce the hide of a hammerhead shark. There was another that had a strange-looking lump at the tip.

"That's compressed air in there," Valar informed them. "The spear passes through the fish, usually a big one, and instantly the compressed air explodes, forcing the end of the spear out into jagged shreds that'll cause concussion and instant death."

Jake picked up one of the compressed-air spears and looked at it carefully. "I wouldn't want a thing like that stuck in me," he said.

Valar smiled. "No, but sometimes we have to protect ourselves and our country by using such weapons."

That night the Sleepers had supper with the king and

the queen and Princess Jere. The elders were not there—only Valar.

"And how are our young friends doing, Valar?" King Cosmos asked.

"Oh, very well, Your Majesty. They've taken to swimming like native Atlantians."

"I'm so glad to hear that." Queen Mab had a sweet smile, but there was a sadness about her that was never quite gone. "But I hate to think about them being subjected to war—so awful."

Cosmos leaned over and patted her hand. "I know, but it must be done, my dear."

Valar said suddenly, "Tomorrow, you'll have a rather unusual day."

Sarah asked at once, "What is it, Valar? Tell us."

Valar shook his head and smiled mysteriously. "You'll find out soon enough."

The next day, they did find out soon enough, for Valar took them to a different air lock. "This lock," he explained, "is where we keep your mounts."

"Mounts? What kind of mounts?" Reb asked with keen interest. "More porpoises?"

"No—" Valar smiled strangely "—a little bit more active than that." He took them over to a chamber and pointed to a porthole. "They're out there in what you might call a corral, I guess, Reb, from what you've told me."

Josh and the other Sleepers crowded to look through the glass, and when they did, Sarah gasped. "But . . . but Valar . . . those are *sharks!*"

"Yes, they are much like a tiger shark." Valar looked at Josh. "Perhaps you'd like to be the first—show the others how it's done?"

Josh could not think of anything he would rather not do than get in the water close to one of those fierce-looking animals with the cruel teeth. But stubbornly he said, "I'll do it. Just show me how."

Valar slapped him on the shoulder. "You're a good mariner, Josh. And it isn't as bad as it looks. These sharks have been specially bred. They will never attack, except as you direct them. They certainly would never attack their own riders. As a matter of fact, we grow quite close to our mounts, much as you grow close to your horses, I suppose, or did back in the old world."

Josh looked again at the shark, wanted to refuse, but there was no way. "Well, we might as well get it over with."

They left the others to watch, and Valar led Josh down to the tank. There they fastened their helmets and entered the underwater corral.

Valar approached one of the huge animals, more than fifteen feet long and sleek as a torpedo. He swam up to the shark, stroked him under the chin, then led him over to a rack where a kind of saddle was hanging. Valar saddled the shark and then motioned for Josh to get on.

Josh did not hesitate, for he knew he'd be lost if he did. Gingerly, he approached the beast, gave himself a push so that he got over the side, and then slipped into the saddle. He found there were pegs inside that he could lock his knees around so that it held him firmly, and there was a sort of bridle. He sat there fearfully, afraid to do anything, while Valar saddled another shark and then came up beside him.

"We'll ride around a little bit, just like riding a horse. Pull right, left, up, or down. Eventually you can just guide them with your knees, when you're familiar enough with your mount."

Josh felt the huge beast quiver beneath him and thought of its great muscles. He thought also of those long teeth, but he nodded, saying, "I'm ready."

"Come along, then."

* * *

Through the porthole the other Sleepers watched Valar show Josh the basics of sharkmanship.

"Yikes," Dave said, "I don't care what he says. If one of those animals had a mind to, he could turn around and bite your head off."

Reb said, "Aw, shoot. That's the same way with a horse. You think about it, now. A horse weighs fifteen hundred pounds, and you weigh a hundred and twenty. All he's got to do is turn around and kick you, and it's all over—but most of them never do."

Dave grinned weakly. "It's that *most of them* I don't like, Reb. They just take one bite, and the show is over."

But that did not happen, and for the next three days the Sleepers worked hard at learning to manage their sharks. They found that there was an art to it but soon learned how.

On the fourth day, Valar said, "Today we're all going fish hunting. I've assigned a man to take each one of you on a hunting trip." He reached out and put his hand on Sarah's shoulder. "I'll take Sarah myself, and the rest of you will have expert mariners to guide you."

Sarah felt Josh's eyes on her but said nothing.

They left almost at once, all heading in different directions, and it was a delightful trip for Sarah. She had been using the spear gun for some time, but the first time a big fish swam by and Valar said, "See if you can hit him, Sarah," she got excited and did not even aim. Unfortunately, she missed the fish by a good five feet and was humiliated.

"That's all right, you'll be fine. You just have to learn to be a little steadier."

Sarah did learn, and before an hour had passed she had shot a beautifully shaped red fish.

Valar said, "These are the best fish, I think, in Atlantis. We'll have him for supper tonight."

Sarah was proud of herself.

For the next hour they hunted but did not take anything more.

It was when they turned to go that it happened. Sarah was slightly behind Valar, who was looking off in another direction. Suddenly, a hideous face appeared in a crevice in a bank of coral, and at once Sarah knew what it was. She had seen this creature in nature films.

A moray eel! her brain cried out, and even as she thought it, the huge eel came exploding out of his hiding place, headed straight for the unprotected Valar.

Without thinking, Sarah raised her spear gun and pulled the trigger. The spear caught the moray eel in the middle of his body. At once, he began to writhe and sank to the bottom.

Valar whirled, saw what had happened, and came back at once. "Good girl!" he exclaimed. "Those things can be nasty."

He said nothing else on the way back. But later that evening, when she was walking along a corridor, looking out the portholes, which she loved to do, he came up to her. "You know, in my country, in Atlantis, when someone saves a life, that life belongs to him."

Sarah felt a thrill run through her, but she said, "I wouldn't know what to do with someone else's life, Valar." She laughed slightly. "I have trouble with my own."

Valar shook his head. "We have a ceremony when someone saves our life." He embarrassed her by kissing her cheek, and then he bowed deeply, saying, "My life is yours."

Sarah flushed. Such a thing had never happened to her before.

What Sarah did not see was that Josh, coming around the turn in the corridor, had seen the last of this episode. Neither did she see the anger on his face as he turned and walked away in the other direction.

* * *

Later that night Sarah encountered Josh. She was still thrilled about what had happened and very happy.

But suddenly he turned and said, "Sarah, you've been so busy with Valar you haven't seen what's going on."

She stared at him angrily. "What do you mean, 'what's going on'?"

"I mean the whole country's falling to pieces. They're ready to give up. The people that are left here are hopeless, and the Council doesn't know how to hold them together. And you're so busy romancing that Valar fellow, you can't see it."

Without another word, Josh stormed off.

That hurt Sarah, for she was fond of Josh, more than any of the other Sleepers. She thought back to the time in the old world when they had become friends, and all the adventures that they had had, and how he'd stood beside her. "I'll have to make it up to him," she said, "but I don't know how."

Later, after supper, Sarah walked along the parapet. She loved to roam the corridors and look out at the sea-green water and the strange animals that cruised by, including whales from time to time. Once she even saw a giant squid. She was still troubled by the encounter with Josh and tried to rationalize it to herself.

She rounded a corner but stopped abruptly when she saw a man standing halfway down the hall. He did not seem to be an Atlantian, and then shock ran through her as she recognized who it really was.

"Goel!" Sarah ran forward and took his hand. He wore his familiar gray cloak. His kind, gray eyes looked down on her, and yet there was a sternness in them.

"Oh, Goel, I'm so glad to see you," she said. "You don't know what's been happening." Then she laughed in confusion. "I don't mean that—of course, you know what's going on."

"Come and walk with me," Goel said. "I have things to say to you."

Afterward, Sarah would never tell anyone all that Goel said on that walk, but the part she remembered best was the last few minutes. He had walked slowly and had told her many things, and her heart felt encouragement and warmth. She wanted to ask him many questions, but finally she settled for one. "Goel, will Atlantis be saved?"

Goel stopped unexpectedly and put his hand on her shoulder. "Yes—if you will help."

Sarah shook her head. "I'm only a girl, not a warrior."

Goel said with a smile, "Don't you know, Sarah, my child? I choose the feeble to overthrow the powerful."

But at that moment Sarah thought of her infatuation with Valar. She whispered, "And Goel, I've been very foolish too."

The smile of Goel was gentle. "All men and all women are foolish at times. The question is, my child, can you receive wisdom?"

"I will try," she whispered.

And then she stood silent while he told her his plan. Finally, he turned and walked away, and she was alone. One cry came from her lips—"But Goel, I can't do it!"

Still, she knew she had no choice but to obey.

7
The Quest

Sarah knew that if she hesitated, thought over what it was that Goel had asked of her, she would never be able to do it. Gritting her teeth, she walked down the hall and knocked on the door where the boys were, then alerted Abbey. When they all came outside, she said, "I've got to talk to you."

Jake asked at once, "What's wrong, Sarah? You're scared, aren't you?"

Sarah could do no more than nod. She said, "Let's go into our room where we won't be interrupted."

As she led them down the hall, she tried to think how to start, but when they were all crowded into the room that she and Abbey shared, staring at her, she knew that there would be no easy way.

She said, "Do you remember once before when you were all asleep and Goel came to me in a dream—or maybe it wasn't a dream—but anyway, he came?"

Abbey said, "I remember that." Cautiously, she watched Sarah, then finally asked, "What is it? Are you trying to tell us that you've seen Goel again?"

"Yes." Sarah looked at Josh and burst out suddenly, "I wish he hadn't come to me. I wish he'd gone to any one of you besides me!"

Josh, for the moment, seemed to have forgotten his irritation with Sarah and said quickly, "Don't be upset, Sarah. Goel speaks to whoever he wants to." He cocked his head to one side and said, "He must have had quite a message to cause you to be as upset as you are."

"I guess you'll all think I'm crazy. It sounds wild even to me, and I don't even know how I can tell you."

Dave stepped up close and patted her shoulder. "You can tell us. After all, we're the Seven Sleepers, aren't we? We're all in this together."

Sarah smiled at him faintly. She needed approval, and Dave's words sounded good. "All right," she said. She hesitated and said plainly, "Goel commands that the seven of us leave Atlantis and that we go to the Citadel of Neptune."

If she had told them that Goel had commanded them to go to the moon, they could not have looked much more shocked.

For one brief moment, Josh just looked at her. "Well, that's fine! We just learned to swim, I'm not even sure I can stay on that blasted shark, and here we've got to go no telling how far, to a place we've never even seen—"

"Don't be like that, Josh," Jake said quickly. He was a small pugnacious boy. Sarah knew he was always ready for an argument, or even a fight, though he rarely won the fights. He set his jaw now and said, "After all, I mean, we don't have any choice, do we? Always before, Goel has brought us through. Why should this be any different?"

Suddenly Josh looked ashamed. "I know. I'm supposed to be a leader of some kind," he said bitterly, "and here I am throwing up arguments. I wish I were a million miles from here. I wish I'd never come to this place. Well, sorry, Sarah. I didn't mean to criticize you—it's just—it seems like a pretty big job."

"I reckon everything Goel handles is a pretty big job," Reb said, "and if he's told Sarah what we're to do, then by gum we'll just do it, somehow."

"Did he say anything else?" Dave demanded.

"Well, he talked a long time, and he said that we'll have to learn through struggle and trial."

"I don't guess he needed to say that." Dave grimaced, "Just the idea of it is a struggle to me. And once we get out there on the bottom of the ocean, out of sight of Atlantis, we can get gobbled up by monsters we never even heard of."

"Yes, and then after we get to the Citadel—if we do—" Josh pondered aloud, "what'll we do? I mean, we just can't go up to the front door and knock politely and say, 'Howdy, Mr. High Lord Admiral! We've come to stop you from invading Atlantis.'" He grinned. "Although that's better than any plan I've got."

For a long time the Seven Sleepers sat around the room, arguing, thinking of plans. As was inevitable, there were arguments about the method.

Abbey brought up one problem. "In the first place, I'm not even sure that the king and queen would let us go."

"Oh, that's another thing Goel said." Sarah spoke up. "I forgot to tell you. We're supposed to go without telling anyone. Not even to leave word where we've gone."

"Well, ain't that a pretty come-off!" Reb slapped his thigh. "I guess that cuts off any thoughts I had about maybe a rescue party coming in case we get in trouble."

Sarah felt terrible. "I'm sorry," she said. "I wish I didn't have to tell you these things—but they're not my idea."

Later on, more serious arguments developed, and as a result Sarah and Josh found themselves heatedly debating about when to try. Josh was for preparing more, learning more about the way, finding the best route to get to the Citadel of Neptune.

"No, we can't do that, Josh," Sarah insisted. "Goel said we were to leave immediately."

Josh frowned. "Right now? We can't do that! We don't even know where we're going."

The argument grew sharper, and finally Sarah, upset and irritated with Josh for his reluctance, said, "We'll take Valar with us as our guide. He knows the way."

As soon as the words were spoken, she was horrified and ready to take back her statement.

But Josh flared up. "Oh, I might have known. Are you telling us that Goel said to take him with us?"

Sarah, already involved over her head, was so angry she said, "Yes, that's what he told me."

"Well, then," Dave said with a sigh, "if we have a guide like that, I guess we'll be all right. I don't mind telling you, it's a relief to me."

A murmur of approval went around the group, and Sarah thought only Josh looked out of sorts. Sarah, because she knew she had lied about Goel's instructions, *felt* out of sorts.

But she said to herself, *Goel knows we don't know the way. He'd want us to have a guide. He knows we'd get lost. We can't go by ourselves. He just didn't tell me that part of it.* On and on she reasoned until finally she had half convinced herself that taking Valar along was what Goel would desire.

Finally Dave said, "I know one thing—we better carry plenty of spears if we want to try to fight our way halfway across an ocean and then try to get inside the Citadel. There's no telling what'll happen."

"There aren't enough spears in this armory to do that job," Josh said. But then he cheered up. "I'll have to admit that I do feel better with a guide."

Ordinarily, this would have cheered up Sarah too, but she was so miserable about the lie she'd told that she sat quietly, saying nothing. Finally, the boys left, and Abbey and Sarah were alone.

Abbey looked wide-eyed at her. "I wish Goel would

come and talk to me sometime," she said. "I wonder why he doesn't?"

"I don't know, but I wish he would too."

"Oh, I'm so glad that Valar is going to be our guide." Abbey gave her a cautious glance, an envious glance. "You know, he's real interested in you, Sarah." She laughed. "I can usually make a boy interested in me, but he acts like you're the only girl around here."

"Oh, there's nothing to that!"

"Yes, there is too. Every time we go anywhere, he's always close to you. Taking us to the Council, going to eat, going on hunting trips. I think he's falling in love with you."

"Oh, that's ridiculous," Sarah said angrily. "I'm too young for such things as that—and he's just a boy himself."

"He won't be a boy always." Abbey snorted. "And you won't be too young always. You know what? I can just see it now! We win the battle with this Aramis, whoever he is, and who is next in line for the throne?"

"Jere, the king's daughter."

"Not likely. I've been talking to some of the people around here, and they want a king, not a queen. And Valar is the closest relative of King Cosmos."

"I guess that's right."

Abbey looked at her, tapped her lower lip in a provocative gesture, and said slowly, "Umm, wouldn't that be something! Wouldn't that be something!"

"Wouldn't what be something?"

"Why, to think—one day Sarah Collingwood may be queen of Atlantis!"

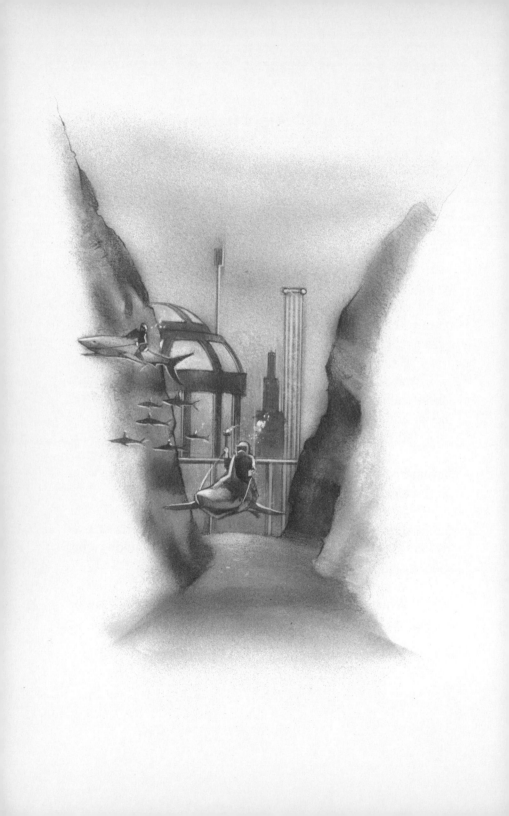

8
First Skirmish

Sarah had restless thoughts. She was very disturbed about telling the group that Valar had been chosen to lead them. But again and again she told herself that Valar was necessary, that Goel would not expect them to go blindly. Finally she managed to shove her unease to the back of her mind and decided to go to Valar at once.

She found him standing at a porthole, watching the guards as they moved back and forth in regular patterns in front of the castle.

"Valar," she said, "I've got to talk to you at once."

He turned, and his eyebrows went up with surprise. "What's the matter? Is something wrong? And why don't you call me Val, as my friends do?"

"No, not wrong—well, perhaps you'll think so." She hesitated, biting her lip nervously. "Val, what do you know about Goel?"

"Goel?" A smile touched his lips, and he shrugged his broad shoulders. "Well, of course, I've heard all the tales and the songs. But I've always thought that Goel was a myth, something that people dreamed up to give them hope."

Sarah shook her head, almost violently. "Oh no, Val," she said. "That's wrong. I've met him. There's nobody like him."

"Well, if you say so, Sarah, then I have to believe it, of course."

"He came to me and told me what we must do."

"He came to you? How could he do that? He couldn't have got past the guards."

"He's bigger than any guards, and no walls could ever keep Goel out. Let me tell you some of the things that he's done . . ."

For a long time Sarah stood there relating the adventures and the dangers that Goel had brought them through. At last she said, "I have to trust him, Val. And I—I have to ask you to do something." She paused. "Goel has given us an order. He says that we are to go to the Citadel of Neptune, and there we're to find Aramis and talk to him face to face."

Surprise crossed the face of the young man, and he whistled softly. "Well, that's a pretty big order. How do you propose to do it?"

"Would—would you guide us to the Citadel, Val? We can't find it unless you do."

His face took on a strange look, and he stood silent for a short time. Then he smiled at her and said, "I would try anything to save my people. Yes, I will lead you to the Citadel."

"Then you do believe in Goel?"

"I believe we have to do something to save Atlantis, and this is all I see to try right now. Come along, we'll have to make our plans."

* * *

It was dark outside as Sarah stared through the porthole. There were artificial lights, yet she could barely see the guards moving back and forth. But they were there, circling the walls constantly.

The Sleepers had met, and Sarah had explained that Val had agreed to guide them. "Maybe," she said, "he could tell us something about how we're going to get there. Would you do that, Val?"

"Of course," he said. "I've brought one of the maps from the war room. Let me show you the problem." He pinned a large map to the wall and stood back so that they could see it. The chart showed the kingdom beneath the sea and included not only Atlantis but also the territory surrounding it.

"Look," he said, "here's where we are in Atlantis. And here"—he pointed to the far side of the map—"is the Citadel of Neptune. That's where Aramis is gathering his forces." He took a deep breath. "We cannot go north. See, that would take us to the Guards of Triton."

"What's that?" Dave inquired.

"It's a large group of mariners that have spread out over this part of the kingdom. And even if we escape them, we would have to pass over the Canyon of Mogar."

"What—what's that?" Abbey asked fearfully.

"It's a deep canyon that goes down to the center of the earth, some say. So deep that there's no light at the bottom—but terrible things are in it. All of us, even the bravest, avoid the Canyon if we can."

"What can we do, then?" Josh asked.

Val pointed. "This is Mount Tor. It's an old volcano, and the tip of it rises above the sea. If we can make it there, we can take shelter for a night."

"What's this hook-shaped thing?" Jake asked.

"That's called Hook Reef. It's a huge coral reef, and it is shaped like a hook, as you see. There's an outpost right here inside the hook, and over to the other side is the Bay of Eels. We don't want to go there, so our best chance," Val concluded, "is to head straight for Mount Tor and try to dodge all the mariners who man the outpost."

He glanced outside. "We'll have to hurry. The guard changes in ten minutes, and that's the only chance we'll have to leave Atlantis."

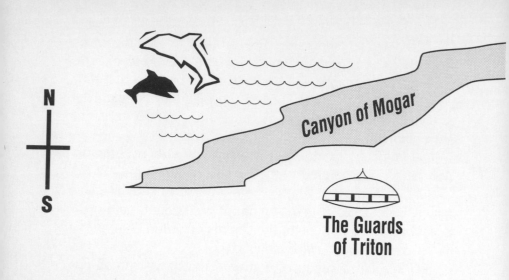

Canyon of Mogar

The Guards
of Triton

The Lost City of Atlantis

Plain of Jadis

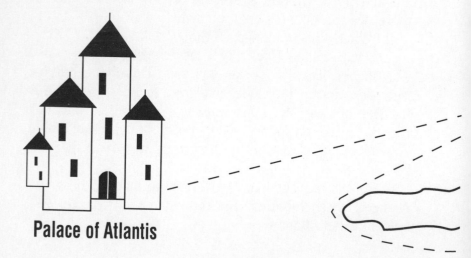

Palace of Atlantis

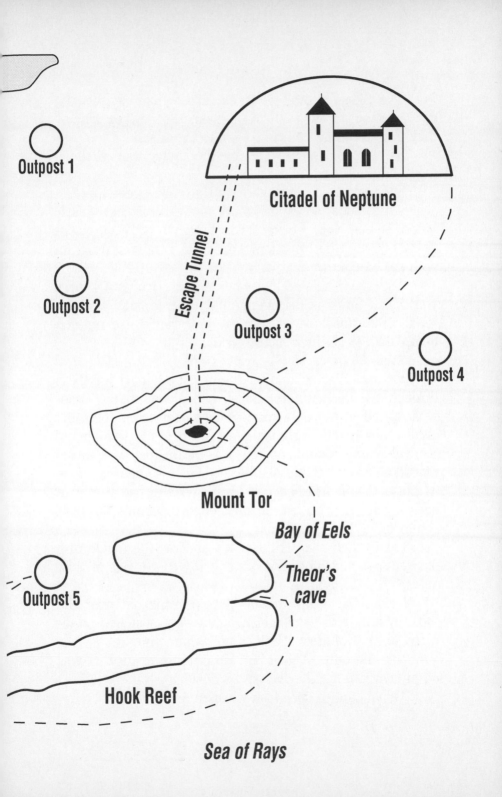

* * *

The Sleepers waited, mounted on their sea beasts, and as soon as Val said, "Come on, it's now or never," they passed through the air lock into the ocean.

Sarah could barely see by the lights that gleamed here and there.

Suddenly a voice called out, "Halt! Who goes there?"

Val at once moved his shark forward, saying, "It's I, Valar. Is that you, Consar? Ah, I see it is. Well, we're going out on a trial mission. Part of the training program with the Sleepers."

The guard saluted and said, "I'd be careful if I were you, Valar. Some of the enemy may be creeping in. We've seen some small patrols around, and they'd like nothing better than to get their hands on you."

"Yes, I'll be careful."

Val moved ahead and for the next two hours led them through the dark waters. Sarah had always been somewhat afraid of the dark, and to be underwater, following almost blindly the single light that Val held up, was almost more than she could bear. She was aware that dark forms moved all around them, sea beasts. Once something came so close that it brushed her arm, and she had to choke back a scream. The rest of the Sleepers seemed no more comfortable than Sarah was.

Finally Reb said, "Shoot, it's dark as the inside of a black cat at midnight. When we going to get out of this, Valar?"

Before Val could answer, a voice rang out over the radio system, and two brilliant lights were switched on directly in front of them. "Halt, stand where you are!"

"It's the outpost guards," Val cried in dismay. "I was off my navigating. They've got us now."

"What can we do?" Josh whispered.

74

"I don't know. But fortunately they can't hear us talking—we're on a different frequency."

As Sarah's eyes became accustomed to the bright light, she saw two guards mounted on large tiger sharks. Both were armed with spear guns, aimed at Val.

"I'll radio back that we've caught some Atlantians," Sarah heard one of them say.

"We've got to get away," Josh repeated.

"They'll spear us if we try," Wash said. "They look like they're just looking for an excuse anyway."

Suddenly Abbey said, "Please, let me try something."

Sarah almost fell off her sea beast in surprise. It was the first time Abbey had ever volunteered to do anything.

"What are you going to do?" she asked.

"I'll . . . I'll fall off my beast, and when they come to get me, you can catch them off guard."

"That may work," Val exclaimed. "But we'll have to act fast. When Abbey falls, one of the guards will go for her. Reb, can you sneak out into the dark and get around behind the other one?"

"Sure as shootin'," Reb said. "Leave it to me."

Abbey slipped from her sea beast at once and began flailing in the dark waters, falling away as she was caught by a current.

"Catch her! One of them has fallen off!" one guard commanded. "Get her, Zantar."

The guard Zantar instantly moved off his shark and propelled himself downward toward Abbey.

As soon as he moved, Reb, who had stayed on the outside of the group, slipped off his beast and propelled himself with powerful strokes into the darkness outside the ring of light thrown by the remaining guard.

"You Atlantians stay right where you are, or I'll put a dart in you," the waiting guard said. "Have you got her?" he called out.

But he said no more, for Reb came up behind him, reached out, and wrenched the spear gun from his hands. He reversed it instantly, touched the needle-sharp tip to the guard's breast, and put his hand on the trigger. "You just sit right there," he muttered, "unless you want be speared like an Arkansas catfish."

The other guard, by this time, reached Abbey, seized her arm, and drove upward. "I've got her—" But suddenly his spear gun was ripped from his hand, and he was pinioned by two strong young men while a young women pointed his own spear gun at him.

"It worked," Val said excitedly, "but we've got to get out of here."

"Won't they know we've been here if these two are missing?"

Val said, "We'll have to kill them. We can't let them take the message back."

"No!" Sarah cried instantly. "We can't do that. Josh always carries cord in his pocket. Let's just tie them up and leave them."

"They might get loose," Val protested. "We can't take the chance."

But Josh swam over beside Sarah and said, "Sarah's right, Val. We can't kill them. Here, Reb," he commanded, "tie them up."

A few minutes later, the two guards were trussed to an outcrop of coral. Josh said as they left, "They'll be all right. The area's under regular patrol, isn't it? The next shift of guards will find them. But by that time we'll be long gone."

Both men stared up at him. They obviously had expected to be killed, and shock was in their eyes as they watched the young group leave, mounted on their beasts.

* * *

76

"Well, that was a close call!" Zantar said. "I looked for them to spear us before they left."

The other looked after them through the gloomy water and said, "Me too. I guess they're not as vicious as we've been told. I'm glad of that. Better to live than to die, isn't it?"

9
"Kill All the Sleepers!"

Many times Elmas, Chief Interrogator of the Sanhedrin, had sent his guards to bring prisoners to the Tower. Often just the threat was enough to make men and women confess. Although most people did not know what went on, the few who came out were never the same again. When asked about what happened inside the Tower, they just turned away. Somehow this silence terrified people even more than knowing the details.

The Tower was operated by Elmas and the Sanhedrin for the purpose of extracting information thought necessary by the leadership. It was also used as a place of punishment for those who were stubborn and refused to obey the Chief Interrogator or his lieutenants.

Elmas was not one of those who did not know what went on. He himself had designed most of the equipment—which was engineered to bring enough pain to cause people to talk—and he had been proud of his success. He had been heard to say, "Why, I've made fathers turn their own children in! I've made wives betray their husbands, and there's nothing that I can't get out of someone once I get him in my Tower."

But it was a shock, to say the least, when Elmas looked up from his desk to see three guards—not his own, but guards bearing the same mysterious crest that was on the medallion hanging from the neck of Lord Necros. Nervously he rose to his feet. "Yes, what is it?"

"You must go with us," the leader said.

They all wore skin-tight black leather uniforms. They

bulged with muscle, and there was a look of cruelty in the eyes of each one.

The heart of Elmas skipped a beat, and he swallowed hard. "Go with you—where?" he almost croaked.

The thin lips of the leader turned up in a cruel smile. "To the Tower." He laughed suddenly. "I don't suppose we'll have to show you the way, will we?"

Elmas began to back away, protesting and stuttering, "But—but—that can't be right! You can't—!"

The guard motioned with his hand, and his companions at once moved forward, each taking an arm of Elmas in his steely grasp.

"Bring him along," the chief guard said, and Elmas was dragged out of his office and down the corridor. His own guards made no motion to interfere but kept their eyes fixed straight ahead. No one interfered with the private guard of Lord Necros.

By the time they had gotten to the steel door that opened into the Tower, Elmas was reduced almost to a gibbering idiot. Fear had turned his insides to jelly, and all he could do was moan and protest. But it did no good.

"Why, you ought to look on this as an opportunity." The chief guard grinned. "After all, you've only had other people's word for how good your 'instruments' are." He moved forward to stand under the chin of the Interrogator and force his head upward. "Now," he said, his eyes shimmering, "you'll be able to explain firsthand exactly how they all work!"

Then the guard's lips became a thin line. "Bring him in. The questioner is waiting."

* * *

Lord Necros stared down at the form that groveled in front of him and then looked up to the guard. "Did the questioner complete his work?"

"Yes, my lord," the chief guard said, his eyes glittering. "I understand that he gave the Chief Interrogator his most careful attention. He assures you that there is nothing that you might wish to know that the man will not tell you."

Lord Necros looked down again. "Look at me, you miserable worm!"

Elmas was not wearing his customary scarlet robe and gold rings on his fingers, the signs of his office. A short garment of rough cloth covered him, reaching to his knees, and when he lifted his face, his eyes were blank. They looked like the eyes of a frightened animal that had been highlighted in a forest. He was shaking all over, as if in a fever, and his lips twitched.

"Now," Necros said harshly, "you have not carried out your promise. The Seven Sleepers have not been recaptured. Every command that I've given you has been broken. Can you tell me any reason why I should not send you back to the questioners?"

Elmas fell on his face again and began pleading, "No, no! please don't send me back there! I will go myself to the Citadel. You will see, sire, it will all be done as you command. I will capture these Sleepers—"

"No, you will remain here." Necros's face was nearly hidden by the heavy cape that almost covered him. His thin lips turned upward in a cruel smile. "I must have you here, Elmas, so that if your latest plan fails, we can see if the questioner can extract a little more from you."

The very mention of such a thing shook Elmas so fiercely that his teeth chattered, and he began to babble, "It will not fail! It cannot fail! We have Lord Aramis completely under our control, and we will capture the Sleepers again, I promise."

Lord Necros glared down at the shaking figure, silence fell over the room, and once again a powerful sense of evil emanated from the Dark Lord. "Your life is forfeit, and your only hope lies in success. I will accept no excuses."

"I . . . I will go at once and contact Duke Lenomar," Elmas said. "May I be dismissed?"

"Go." Lord Necros motioned with a strong hand. "When I hear from you again, I trust to hear better news."

* * *

Duke Lenomar stood holding the message that had just been brought to him. He recognized the special lieutenant of Elmas the Chief Interrogator, his master, and said, "Wait. I will see if there is to be an answer."

He scanned the words quickly and froze as the messenger watched furtively.

Duke Lenomar kept his eyes on the paper for a long time. He was a handsome man with dark eyes and dark hair, who wore the symbol of authority in a medallion around his neck. He had made himself indispensable to Lord Aramis, and now, in many cases, he exerted the power that that young man had once wielded.

Finally looking up, he said, "Take this answer back to Lord Elmas. Tell him that all shall be done as he commands."

"Yes sir," the messenger said. Doubt came to his eyes, and he hesitated. "I think it would be well if you succeed, sir. If not, Lord Necros has a long arm. He can reach, I think, even down here to the Citadel of Neptune."

"Begone!"

Duke Lenomar watched the messenger turn on his heel and leave the room. He frowned and began pacing back and forth. Thoughts ran through his head and were reflected on his swiftly changing features. He was a man of tremendous intelligence, he was accustomed to power, and he had moved upward in the kingdom of Atlantis from a low post to the second highest in the land. He had even greater plans for when Aramis retook the kingdom, but these he kept to himself.

At last he reached a decision. In quick, firm strides he left his quarters and made his way through the Citadel, crossing many passageways, until he came to a door guarded by two sentries, who eyed him sternly.

The duke gave the password that even he must give, and the guards opened the doors. Passing through them, Duke Lenomar saw Aramis standing before a map of the kingdom. He approached and said cautiously, "My Lord Aramis . . ."

Aramis turned, his blue eyes coming at once to rest on Lenomar. "What is it?"

"The Sleepers, my lord. I must speak to you of them."

Aramis moved over to a black chair positioned in front of the map, sat down in it, and ran his hand over his blond hair. Even in repose, he looked strong, this Lord Admiral. At twenty-five, he had lived enough for several men's lifetimes. But restlessness and confusion were in his voice as he said, "They are not dangerous."

"I do not think, my lord Aramis, that you recognize how powerful these young people are."

"How can they be powerful? There are only seven of them, and the oldest of them is a mere boy. What can they do to a kingdom such as this—to a force such as mine?"

Duke Lenomar bit his lip. He had been through this before with Aramis but now knew that he must make him understand. "My lord, strength does not always lie in the heaviest battalions. Sometimes there are strange things that cannot be explained, for the world we inhabit is not only physical, but spiritual."

Aramis put his gaze on Duke Lenomar, studying him. There was a quick intelligence in his eyes, despite the cloudiness that seemed to haunt them. "I did not know you believed in the gods."

"I believe in force," Lenomar answered rapidly, "and somehow there's power in these Sleepers. They managed to escape all the forces of the Sanhedrin, did they not? We know that much about them. Anyone who can escape my lord Elmas is not a fool. These seven young people are somehow tied in with destiny. I know it. And their destiny is to destroy us. Therefore, my lord, we must find them and kill them."

Still Aramis hesitated. At last he said, "They did not kill our guards. Why was that?"

"I cannot answer that." Lenomar hesitated. "But one act does not negate their mission. They are sent by the one called Goel to establish the kingdom of King Cosmos—this much we know."

"Goel." Lord Admiral Aramis said the name slowly. "Who is this Goel? Is he the same as in the myth that I've heard—and the songs—'the House of Goel will be built'?"

"My lord, you are not well," Duke Lenomar said. "Trust my judgment in this."

There was a long discussion between the two, and the longer it went on, the more Lenomar became alarmed. Aramis, he saw, was slipping from his control.

Aramis said wistfully, "Sometimes, Duke, I think I was wrong to lead this revolt. I know you counseled me to do so, but my mind is troubled over it."

I've got to put him under stricter control, Lenomar thought. Quickly he crossed to a cabinet, pulled out a bottle, filled a glass. Keeping his body between his hand and the admiral, he slipped his fingers into his inner pocket, drew out a small glass vial, and managed to pour several drops of liquid into the drink. Then he turned and brought the glass to Aramis. "Drink this, my lord."

Aramis frowned. "I do not need medicines."

"You are weaker than you thought. The pressures," Lenomar urged, "have been terrible. All the destiny of our people rests on you, and you are tired. This will help you to rest. I know you have not slept."

Aramis hesitated, then took the goblet. "You're right, I've not slept. I'm troubled about all of this, Lenomar, very troubled." He stared at the drink, then shrugged his wide shoulders and drank it down. Handing the glass to the duke, he leaned back in his chair and grew quiet.

Lenomar replaced the goblet and returned to stand to the right of the admiral. He waited for some time, speaking of inconsequential things, and then he put his hand lightly on the blond head of Aramis and began to whisper, "You are sleepy—you are very sleepy. You are falling asleep." He continued for perhaps three minutes, then saw with satisfaction that the admiral had indeed fallen asleep, his head resting against the back of the chair.

Now Lenomar moved behind the young man and again put his hand on his head. His voice grew deeper, and he began to repeat certain phrases over and over again rhythmically. "King Cosmos is evil—he will destroy Atlantis—you are the rightful ruler." Over and over again he said these things, and then, "The Sleepers must die—the Sleepers must die—the Sleepers must die. And when all is done, Lord Necros will make you king of Atlantis, but the Sleepers must die."

Aramis sat there stiffly. Finally, when the voice of Duke Lenomar paled, he opened his heavy eyes and whispered, "The Sleepers must die. King Cosmos is evil. The Sleepers must die."

Lenomar smiled and went at once to the door. Opening it, he spoke to one of the guards. "Lord Aramis has a message that must be sent to all units."

"Yes sir, I will take it myself."

"Lord Aramis commands that every available mariner

be sent to search for those called the Sleepers. They must be found."

"Yes, my lord." The guard nodded obediently. "And what shall be done with them, sir? Shall they be brought here to the Citadel?"

"No!" The dark eyes of Lenomar gleamed, and he said in a chill voice, "Kill them! When you find them, kill them at once. This is the order of the Lord Admiral Aramis!"

10

Monsters of the Deep

W e'll have to go around Hook Reef," Valar said grimly. "It's a dangerous place, but we've got to get away from the guards. They'll be coming this way any time."

"Can't we just go straight on through to the Citadel?" Josh asked.

Val shook his head, his mouth clenched tight. "There's no hope at all that way. There are outposts strung in front of it, and the guards fan out in all directions." He said roughly, "We don't have as much chance now as we did. We've set the alarm off, and you can be sure that Aramis is smart enough to close the gates. Are you sure you don't want to turn back?"

"No," Josh said quickly. "We can't do that."

"There's a difference between courage and foolhardiness," Val said. "We don't have much chance, whichever way we go."

"But Goel told us what we're to do," Sarah said. "He's never led us wrong. Please—" she put her hand on Val's arm "—please, let's try. We've got to do our best."

Val shrugged. "All right, but if you remember the map, we're up close to the top of the Hook now. We'll have to go back to the shank, go around, and come up the other side." He hesitated. "I have to tell you, they call that area on the south side of Hook Reef the Sea of Rays."

"That sounds nice," Abbey said. "You mean like rays of the sun?"

"No, I mean like giant stingrays."

Wash's eyes popped open. "You mean them big things that look like bats? I've seen them on TV."

"You haven't seen any like these," Val said. "These are not just stingrays. Some of those, in the old days, got to be as much as three or four feet across, some of them even larger. But—"

"You mean—" Jake stared at him "—you mean these are bigger than that?"

"I mean some of them are fully fifteen feet across, wing tip to wing tip."

The group just looked at him. Dave finally swallowed hard and said, "What about stingers? Do they have those too?"

"Worse than anything you ever heard of," Val said gloomily. "It's kind of like a dart, and a sting would be bad. They go right through a diving suit. The suits automatically seal, but unless you get to a doctor real quick, you're a goner." He looked around. "Maybe we'd better take a vote about whether to go on or not."

"No," Josh said grimly, "we've all decided to go on to the Citadel. This is just going to make it harder, that's all." He looked at Val. "We're in your hands, I guess, and I'll follow wherever you lead."

Val smiled then. "Well, I'll try to get us through, but let's hope we don't run into a swarm of giant rays."

He led out again, and by the time they had reached the eastern side of Hook Reef and turned back west, Wash and Reb rode close together. Josh heard Reb say, "You know, it's downright pretty down here, ain't it? Everything's all in Technicolor."

Everybody knew Wash was still afraid of water, but as he looked about at the swarms of red, yellow, and purple fish, some of them bigger than the Sleepers themselves, Wash said, "I'd like to get a picture of all this." As they moved on, he asked, "Are you scared, Reb?"

"I don't know. I'd hate to tell you if I was."

Wash said, "Shoot, I ain't afraid. Oh, well . . . maybe a little. But we'll be OK."

They moved along the reef. Josh too was conscious of the brilliant colors of all sorts of animal life. He had never dreamed that a reef was so busy nor had he ever seen such weird, fantastic formations.

They had gone for almost an hour when Val said, "All right. This is where the Sea of Rays begins. Keep a lookout."

They gathered in a group to have more firepower.

"This is kinda like pulling the wagons around in circles, ain't it?" Reb said. "That's the way they did it out West. Then the Indians would gallop around but couldn't get at them, they were all so close."

"Well, if you ask me," Jake said, his eyes darting about nervously, "I think these rays Val's talking about are worse. The Indians didn't have stingers in their tails, anyway."

On and on they swam. The shark sea beasts moved beneath them effortlessly. At one point Val led them down deeper, saying, "Less current to fight down here."

Only a few moments later, he cried, "Look out, there they come! See—over there!"

Josh saw overhead a group of huge, shadowy stingrays approaching. They looked like great bats, their wings moving slowly.

"Stop," Val said. "Be absolutely still. Maybe they won't see us."

The Sleepers drew up their beasts and grouped as close together as they could. For a moment Josh thought the monsters overhead would pass, but suddenly one of them veered downward.

"They've seen us," Jake yelled. "Here they come!"

"Get ready," Val commanded. "Load your guns."

89

Josh grabbed a compressed-air dart, loaded it, waited, and saw that the others had done the same.

The first ray came fluttering down, the stinger in his tail twitching back and forth, as if it belonged to a huge cat.

"Don't everybody fire. We'll have to fire volleys so that when some of us are reloading, the others are still armed," Val yelled. "Jake, you and Wash and I are one group, the rest of you the other group. Get ready, and the first group will fire."

The rays swam above them like great birds. "That's what they do," Val said. "They get down on top of you and smother you. Get ready, they're all hitting at once. One— two—three—fire!"

Jake, Wash, and Val fired quickly—the first beast was only ten feet away—and all three spears sank in its midsection, penetrated hide, and went off with a muffled sound Josh heard even through the water. The ray suddenly flipped over. Writhing wildly, it tried to swim away but had gone no more than twenty feet when it began to sink, absolutely motionless.

"Here comes the rest of them," Reb yelled. "Our turn now."

Josh yelled, "You and Dave take that one on the right, and we'll take the other two."

The giant ray began to settle as the spears flew upward. Unfortunately two missed, and it was Val with his group who had reloaded who were able to drive the others off.

Val was the hero of the hour. "Stay together, fire volleys, wait till they get down right over us, but watch out for those stingers."

That was exactly what they could not do. Three big rays came in at once, and while the Sleepers killed two of

90

them, the other one suddenly covered Reb, who had moved off to one side.

Frozen with fear, Josh saw the stingray settling down on his friend.

Reb reached up and tried to shove the huge, rough beast away. It didn't work. Then Reb turned his compressed-air gun toward the stingray's leathery stomach.

"Here she goes!" Reb cried.

The dart fired off, drove into the beast's middle, but apparently at such an angle that the ray was only wounded. It turned and began to flutter away, and then the wildly twitching tail suddenly collided with Reb's right leg.

Josh left his sea beast and swam quickly down. "Are you all right, Reb?" But Reb's eyes were turned upward in his head, showing only the whites.

"Got to get him out of here!" Grabbing Reb's arm, he pulled him back to the group and found that the rest of the rays seemed to have been discouraged and were slowly withdrawing, their huge wings moving slowly.

"Reb got hit by a stinger. We've got to help him."

Val shook his head. "We'll have to get him out of here. And the only place to go is up on the eastern side of the island. It's called Theor's Cave. Can you tie him into the saddle? Maybe we can make it."

They worked quickly getting Reb tied into the saddle, and Josh and Dave rode on each side to be sure that he didn't fall off.

"Come on," Val said, "we've got to make it as quick as we can. The poison works fast."

They drove their sea beasts to the limit of their speed, but still it was an hour before they turned north. Five minutes later, Val led them into what seemed to be a wall of solid rock.

"Here," he said. "This cave moves upward and has an air space in it. Hurry!"

Josh held Reb, who had become totally helpless.

As they entered the cave there was darkness, but then they emerged into an above-water cavern.

"Hang on. I know where the lights are," Val called out. He had switched on his own light, such as they all carried, and quickly moved out of sight. "Just like an underground river," he said, hurrying back. "We'll tether the beasts here. Bring him up on the shore."

Dave and Josh carried the limp form of Reb up onto the beach and laid him down.

"What is this place?" Sarah asked, looking around. It was not a large cave, probably no more than forty feet in diameter, but obviously it had been built, for the walls were not rough coral, but smooth.

"We made it for a tidal wave, or in case anybody ever got lost or trapped in enemy territory. See," Val said, "there's food stored here, and we can make a fire."

"Let's do it. Reb's cold," Josh said. He pulled Reb's helmet free and felt his forehead. "He's freezing to death."

Soon they had made a fire out of materials left in one of the lockers, and it made the place a little more cheerful. They stripped the diving suit off Reb and wrapped him in blankets they found stored in another locker, but he was absolutely motionless.

"Can't we do anything else for him?" Sarah pleaded. She was holding Reb's head in her lap and was frightened at the absolute stillness of his body.

"It's the poison," Val said. "Most people die when they get hit by a ray that big."

"No," Sarah cried out. She held the boy's head closely. "We've got to do something. He can't die!"

Val's face was grim. "Everybody dies." He looked upward and added tightly, "We'll all die if Aramis takes us."

They made a quick meal out of the food that had been stored. No one was hungry, but they all tried to eat something.

Josh and Sarah stayed close to Reb, and Wash took up his position by the boy's side and held his hand. "Ain't we going to do something?" he begged. "We can't let him die like this."

Sarah looked at Josh, who said, "I'd do anything I could, but who could know about a thing like this?"

Sarah said suddenly, "I wish we'd never come. I wish you'd never listened to me."

Josh moved closer and put a hand on her shoulder. "You can't blame yourself, Sarah. We came at Goel's command. That's all we could do, and we've got to keep on going, no matter what happens. Even if—"

He suddenly broke off. He had intended to say "even if Reb dies."

Sarah looked down at Reb's pale face. "I don't know what to think anymore. I don't know how to talk or how to ask Goel for help or anything else." There was desperation in her voice. She lowered her head and began to weep.

Josh, feeling self-conscious, put his arm around her and drew her close. "I guess we all feel that way," he said. He held her for a long time.

Finally she cried herself out, and then she looked up at him with a tired smile. "You do have a time with me, don't you, Josh Adams?"

He was embarrassed by the question. "Oh, I don't know." The two sat there with Wash as the time went on, and with each moment it seemed Josh could see life leaving the still form of Reb Jackson.

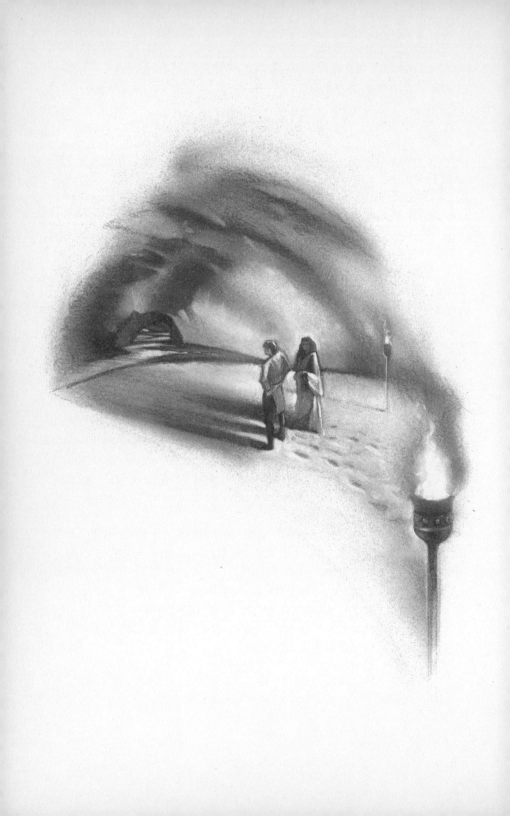

11

If I Were King

For hours Sarah and her friends took turns watching the sick boy. At times he would appear to wake up, but he never spoke anything resembling logical speech. A raging fever took him, and they had to bathe him with cold cloths to fight it down until it was not deadly.

Val stared down at him. "There's only one thing that would help," he said hesitantly.

"What is it?" Josh said. "Anything we can do?"

Val shifted nervously, locked his hands behind his back and said, "There is one sort of medicine, but it's very rare and hard to find."

"Isn't there any in the locker?" Sarah asked.

"No, although there should be. It's made from a particular kind of coral, a soft coral. Very hard to find."

Josh said, "Well, we're in a coral reef. Is there some of it here?"

"Yes, I suppose there is," Val said. "But if we go out there—in the first place, those rays are there. In the second place, if Aramis has his mariners out searching for us, we run the chance of being found."

"I don't care," Sarah said. "We've got to go find some of it."

Josh said, "Tell me what it looks like. I'll go."

But Val shook his head. "You'd never find it, Josh. And if you did, you probably couldn't find your way back here."

Sarah was waiting for Val to offer to go, but the young man merely turned and walked down to the beach, where he stood staring moodily into the still, green waters.

"I'll go talk to him," Sarah said. "You stay with Reb, Josh."

"All right, I will."

Val turned to meet her. There was a strange look on his face, and he appeared to be more sober and thoughtful than usual. He stared at her as she began to speak, telling him how she would do anything—she would go herself.

"Just tell me what it looks like—we've got to try something."

Val pressed his lips firmly together. Finally he said, "It's not that I'm afraid to go—although it is dangerous—but I can't."

"Why not, Val? He's going to die if we don't get help."

"He may die anyway. That was a huge ray that got him, and he took a big dose of the poison. I'm not sure that he would live even if we got help, even if we got the medicine."

"But we can't just let him die." Sarah's eyes pleaded with Valar. She came closer. "He's such a fine boy, and he's been through so much. Please, Val, help us."

There was a long silence, as Val turned back toward the sea and appeared to forget about her. Sarah could do nothing but wait. Finally, he wheeled around and said, "I had a dream last night."

"But what has that to do—"

"You've told me several times about your dreams, that Goel appears to you and tells you what to do. Isn't that right?"

"Yes, of course. It's happened more than once. And not just to me, but to Josh as well, and the others."

Val rubbed his forehead, covering his eyes for a moment. "I never believed much in dreams. At least I never

96

believed they meant anything. But while I was dozing a little while ago, I had one. Never had anything happen to me like that before. It was real."

"What was it? What did you see?"

"Well, I didn't see anything, but I heard something—a voice. I don't know whose voice it was, but it said, 'You are the closest to the throne, and when Aramis is gone, you are of the royal blood and will rule over Atlantis.'"

Sarah stared at him. "I don't know what that means."

"Why, it means what it says, Sarah. Didn't you know that I'm the nephew of King Cosmos, the only living male heir to the throne? Aramis has gone. He probably would have been king, but he's forfeited that now. His rebellion has cut him off forever from the throne."

Sarah listened to the waves lap the sandy beach. She was shocked by what she had heard, although really she had known it. "What would you do if you were king?"

"If I were king? First, I'd execute all the traitors and the rebels. Kill this rebellion dead in its tracks."

"But a ruler should be kind, shouldn't he?"

"I could be that too." Val smiled. "There's a time for each, isn't there? I mean, in a war when you're fighting to save your country, is there really any way to be kind?"

"No, no, I suppose not. Though I hate the thought of it. But Reb—"

"You Sleepers," Val said suddenly, "are very important." He suddenly reached out and took her by the shoulders, asking, "Can you do magic?"

"No, of course not!" Sarah said. She was embarrassed by the question, and somehow the touch of his hands was sending a sort of strange signal to her, something she had never felt before. He was so tall, so fine looking, and his eyes burned as he looked at her.

"Nevertheless, you are the key," Val said. "Cosmos said so. And anyway, you would not be hunted by Lord

97

Necros if you were not. You must play some part in what's going on in Atlantis."

"I've never understood it," Sarah said. She was still very conscious of his hands on her arms. She wished that he would remove them and yet at the same time that he would leave them there, strangely enough. "I think that somehow we've been brought to this time and place to bring the House of Goel into being—at least to help—but none of us have ever known exactly what we were to do."

Val stood there thinking, and his grip on her arms increased. "We will help each other," he said finally.

"How?" Sarah whispered.

"I will get the medicine for your friend. That will prove to you that I care, and that I am loyal. If I risk my life, will you believe that?"

"Oh yes, Val," she whispered. "I would believe that."

He looked down at her, and there was a light in his eyes. "Sarah, when the time comes, you will help me. I will need your support."

"Of course, you'll be the lawful ruler of Atlantis," Sarah whispered.

"No, I mean more than that." He hesitated. "You and I, Sarah, we will rule together, king and queen."

Shock roared through Sarah's head, and she thought she had misunderstood him.

But he said, "We will marry. *We* will rule Atlantis."

"I'm too young," Sarah cried out.

A smile touched Val's lips. Very gently he pulled her forward, held her in his arms, and leaned over and kissed her cheek. Then he released her so that she stepped back, fear in her eyes but also something more than that.

"You are young. And so am I, but one thing is certain, Sarah."

"What is that, Val?"

"We are young, but time will change that. We will win this revolution, and time will go on, and we will learn to love each other—not as children, but as man and woman."

He turned and walked away, calling to the others as he pulled on his diving suit. "I will try to find the medicine that will help our friend. All of you stay here until I come back." When he had the suit on, he quickly mounted his sea beast and disappeared in a swirl of water.

Josh came over and asked curiously, "What did you do to get him to go, Sarah?"

Sarah shook her head. "Nothing, Josh, nothing at all." And then suddenly she began to sob and walked away from him without speaking.

* * *

Josh stared after her, wondering. *I never will learn to understand that girl.*

12
Wash's High Hour

After Val left, the others tried to get some rest, but Wash stayed beside Reb, his eyes fixed constantly on his friend's face. For a long time Reb did not move at all, and the smallest of the Seven Sleepers grew more and more despondent. He closed his eyes and was saying a prayer to Goel when all of the sudden a faint voice said, "Hey, what you doin' there, Wash?"

Wash's eyes flew open, and he saw that Reb was moving his head and watching him.

Wash leaned forward and took Reb's hand. "You're awake. Hey, it's good to see you come out of it."

Reb blinked slowly, and the usual cheerful spirit was gone. "I guess . . . not out of it yet. Never felt so bad, not even when I had malaria."

Wash squeezed the limp hand in his and worked up a smile. "You're gonna be all right. Mr. Valar, he's gone to get you some medicine that's gonna get you all well again."

Reb smiled faintly. "Sure do hope so, Wash, sure do. I'd hate to know I'm gonna feel this bad the rest of my life."

The two of them were silent for a long time. Occasionally Wash said a word to establish communication. Finally, Reb looked up out of hollow eyes, and a faint grin touched his lips. "This is funny, about you and me being friends, ain't it, Wash?"

Wash knew instantly what the boy meant. "You mean about us being different colors? I guess that's one good thing about coming to Nuworld—I found me one good friend."

Reb grinned faintly at him. "Yep, good old . . . Wash . . ."

He faded off, and Wash leaned back and began again to ask Goel for help.

* * *

Sarah awoke to find that Josh was awake too. They lay there listening to the water lapping on the sand, from time to time casting a glance over to where Wash sat beside the wounded boy. Finally, Sarah said, "Josh . . ."

"Yes, what is it, Sarah?"

"Do you ever doubt?" Then she said quickly, "I mean, all the jams we've gotten into and now this one. Do you ever just wonder if there's anything to it all?"

"You mean Goel and the House that he's talking about, and are we going to get out of this?"

"Yes." Sarah rolled over and looked into his eyes, "Don't you sometimes just wonder if we're not kidding ourselves?"

"Sure, don't you?" He caught her nod and said, "You know, it's pretty easy to believe when things are going fine, but when we're in a mess like this, I guess that's what really tests whether we believe or not."

Sarah nodded, "I believe in Goel but . . . I don't know—somehow being in this cave, and Reb may be dying over there, and no way that I can think of to get into the Citadel, it just looks pretty grim right now."

Josh sat up, crossed his legs, and put his elbows on his knees, holding his chin. He was quiet for a while, but finally he said, "You remember the stories my mother used to read to us after you came to live with us?"

"Yes, I remember that."

"Well, if you think about it, those fellows in those

stories had some pretty dark times too. Just think about old Jonah—at least we're not in some whale's belly. We'd have a hard time cooking a meal up in a thing like that, wouldn't we?"

"Why, that's silly, Josh." Sarah smiled, glad that he was talking.

"I don't think it's silly. Remember Daniel? He was all set to be a prophet sandwich for a bunch of lions, but he never did doubt. Do you remember?"

"Yes, I remember." They talked on and on about men and women who endured in dark, hard places, facing death. Somehow Sarah felt the better for it. Then their conversation was interrupted when Dave sang out, "Look, there comes Val."

They all came to their feet and rushed down to meet Valar. The young man slipped off his sea beast, waded in to the shore, and grinned at them. Holding up a sack, he said, "I got it."

Sarah ran and threw her arms around him. "Oh, Val, I knew you'd do it."

Val hugged her and said, "Well, all we have to do is get some water boiling and dissolve this stuff in it. Come on, you girls, let's see some action!"

An hour later, they had cooked the coral down until it made a soupy pot full of liquid.

"What do you do with it? Does he swallow it?" Sarah asked.

"No, you put it on the puncture," Val said, "and you keep it moist. I know that much."

At once, Sarah bent over Reb and drew the cover off his leg. The leg was swollen, and around the puncture wound was a blackish, angry-looking area. Sarah dipped out some of the medicine and put it on her finger.

"We'll take turns. We'll keep that stuff on him at all times," Josh said.

103

* * *

"Well, it worked," Val said with satisfaction. He was sitting off to one side and looking over to where Reb was propped up, laughing and talking and eating. "Took twenty-four hours, but I guess that's pretty quick for medicine to work."

"Oh, Val, I'm so happy," Sarah said. She put out her hand, and he took it and squeezed it. "I'm so thankful to you, and all the rest of us are too."

"I'm glad I could help." Valar thought for a moment and asked, "What do you think it was? Your prayers to Goel or my going out and getting the coral? Couldn't I have gone and gotten the medicine without prayers?"

"Oh, I think prayer and action sometimes are all tied together," Sarah said. "We pray and then we do all we can and are obedient to Goel, and that's all I know to do."

Val stared at her, an odd expression in his eyes, and said, "Well, we're all in this together, aren't we?" He squeezed her hand again. "The king and the queen?"

Sarah flushed and lowered her eyes, pulling her hand back. She said, "Don't tell anyone about that. Will you promise, Val?"

"Of course not," he said. "That's just our secret."

* * *

Reb improved almost hourly, and twenty-four hours later they were ready to go.

Valar said as they were preparing, "I'll go up and take a look, to be sure no patrols are around."

The others were pulling their belongings together when all of the sudden Sarah heard a furious splashing. She looked up to see Val coming out of the air lock, his arms flailing, pulling at his mask.

104

"What's wrong? What is it, Val?" Sarah cried as they all rushed to him.

Val's eyes were wide with shock. He pointed to his right arm and said, "Look at that."

She looked down at Val's right arm and saw a series of red rings that had pulled the fabric loose.

"There's a giant squid—a huge octopus—and he's perched right outside the cave," Val whispered. "He nearly got me. If he'd gotten one more tentacle on me, I'd be dead by now."

"Come on, we'd better get that suit patched up and that arm treated," Josh said.

Val let them lead him back close to the fire where they repaired the suit and examined his wounds.

The sucker marks were not serious, but Val was shaken. "Those things can wait around for days," he moaned.

"Maybe not," Dave said hopefully. "Maybe he'll get tired and go on."

Val jerked his arm back from Sarah, who was attempting to put some ointment on the sucker marks, and gritted his teeth. "He won't. We're lost now. I wish I'd never got pulled into this crazy scheme."

His words shocked Sarah. She thought none of them had considered anything other than going on.

Wash said, "We're gonna make it, Mr. Val. Goel ain't brought us this far to let us down now."

"You don't know these squid. None of you do. They're just patient as a mountain and can stay in one place about that long. Once they get a hint about a prey—which is us—they'll stay forever. And the only way out of this cave is right past that monster."

Dave said, "Well, it's a bad scene all right, but I'm believing somehow we'll get out of it."

"You can believe in anything you want," Val said, "but what I'd like is for about a battalion of good mariners to suddenly appear and fill that thing so full of darts he'd shrivel up. It's a big one too. I've never seen a larger octopus."

Val walked away from the group and stood staring moodily out at the water. The others milled about, not knowing what to do.

At last Sarah said, "Well, seems like we've been here before, doesn't it? Come to the end of everything. Remember how we thought we'd come to the end when all those soldiers of the Sanhedrin were coming and all we had was a stone wall that we couldn't get by?"

"That's right," Josh agreed, "and Goel brought us through that. He'll get us through this too."

Though they talked as cheerfully as they could, Sarah saw that none of them actually had much faith. Finally they ate a little, although no one seemed very hungry, and went to bed.

* * *

Wash moved over close to Reb, and they talked for a while.

Reb said, "Well, I know one thing, I don't believe in going down with your bat on your shoulder."

"You mean, we ought to go out and tackle that thing out there?"

"Probably wouldn't make it, according to what Val says," Reb said, "but I sure hate to go out doing nothing."

"You know," Wash said, "everybody's done something for the group—everybody but me."

"What do you mean by that?" Reb demanded.

"I mean Josh, and Sarah, and Dave, and you, and Abbey—everybody has gotten us out of a mess at one time or another." He stared down at his hands and looked very small as Reb glanced at him. "But I haven't ever done anything to help us."

Reb reached over and punched his shoulder. "Don't you worry about that. We're all one. It doesn't matter who does the work as long as we all stick together."

Reb was still weak from his fever and said, "I think I'll take a little nap." He lay back and was asleep almost instantly, but he could not sleep long. There was a rock under his shoulder, and he rolled over to remove it. As he did, his eyes opened. He sat up abruptly, staring around. "Wash. Wash?"

From across the way, Dave called out, "What is it? What's wrong, Reb?"

"It's Wash. He's gone!"

Everyone came rushing over and saw that Reb had spoken the truth.

Val took in the situation. Quickly he went to where the equipment was stashed. "His spear gun's gone." He looked toward the water. "You know, I think he went out to tackle that giant squid."

"Oh no," Sarah moaned, "he'll be killed."

"Probably already is," Val said. "Poor little guy, I could have told him that nobody ever wins in a one-man battle with a monster that big."

* * *

Slowly, Wash moved along through the canal to the opening of the cave. He was trembling, but he held his spear gun as firmly as he could with both hands. He remembered what Val had taught them, so he had loaded the gun with six compressed-air darts and had set the trigger to automatic, which meant as soon as he pulled it, the six darts would be fired, one after the other, in a matter of seconds.

It's kind of like a machine gun, he thought as he moved forward, paddling with his fins. He felt very much alone, and fear almost paralyzed him. But he kept repeating, *Goel, let me do something to help my friends. Help me kill this big old scudder.*

The tunnel was dark, but he saw up ahead a glimmer of light—the entrance to the cave. Even as he watched, several long objects moved in front of the opening, and he knew that they were the tentacles of the octopus.

He'd once seen a movie about a giant squid that had attacked a ship, pulled the sailors off, and killed them one at a time. Wash fully expected this would happen to him. But he forged on anyhow, hopeless yet remembering that Goel had done many marvelous things in the past.

He edged up to the opening. Even as he did, the tip of a tentacle slid inside and moved like a huge snake down the tunnel. The octopus was reaching into the cave, feeling for its prey. On and on it went until the body of the octopus blocked the opening. The tentacle, at its heaviest part, Wash saw, was a foot or more across. He knew the body of the thing must be enormous.

Got to get him in the belly, Wash thought desperately. He watched as the tentacle felt about the cave, touching, searching, like a long, enormous finger.

Then Wash blotted out all thought of what it would be like to be clasped by those enormous feelers and have its suckers all over him. He knew that once he fell into the grasp of that mighty beast, he was lost. He paddled forward, barely moving his fins, careful not to touch the tentacle. Something about his movement caused the tentacle to suddenly writhe, though, and to Wash's horror it withdrew until the end of it, moving about the cave, touched his arm. He jerked back in terror, but before he could escape, the tentacle had wrapped itself around his body.

The pressure was enormous, and he felt the power of the monster. He felt also that he was being drawn toward the opening of the cave.

Just give me one shot! Help me get it right!

When he cleared the opening, all Wash could see was the massive body and the huge staring eyes of the awful, misshapen beast. The water had filled with writhing tentacles that all began to move toward him. He saw that he was underneath, and he saw the huge mouth that would tear him to pieces. It opened wide to receive him, and Wash now knew what death was.

Other tentacles began to enclose his arms and his legs.

Wash raised the dart gun, pointed it straight at the soft underbelly of the beast and, with a prayer to Goel, pulled the trigger. The gun bucked in his hand, but he held it steady.

Then he saw the darts—all six of them—penetrate the body of the octopus and disappear, buried deep. There was a series of muffled sounds as the expanding air exploded and literally blew the monster to pieces. For one moment, the tentacles pulled at him, probably a reflex action, and then they grew limp. Instantly Wash kicked himself free and back into the cave, his heart beating like a trip-hammer.

"I done done it!" he cried aloud. "I done killed that big old suckcr!"

He swam as quickly as he could back down the tunnel, ducked under the air lock, and came up. He saw the others walking aimlessly around, and he pulled his helmet off and shouted, "Hey, it's me. I done killed that big old critter!"

His friends ran to him, and the cave was filled with the cries and shouts of excitement.

109

And then, as he told them what he had done, Val nodded with admiration. "You ought to get a medal for that. Nobody's ever done it before."

Dave and Josh picked up the small boy on their shoulders and began carrying him around in a victory celebration.

And as the others watched and cheered, Wash said under his breath, "I sure wish my momma could see me now!"

13

To the Gates of Neptune

After Wash's victory over the giant squid, all the Sleepers were filled with confidence. Val was very impressed, but he shook his head. "Well, it was a marvelous thing," he said, "and one that will be sung in many songs, but we're not to the Citadel yet."

"What do we do now?" Josh asked.

Val bit his lip and thought hard. Finally he said, "We'll stick with our original plan. We're going to Mount Tor." He hesitated, then smiled. "You ought to like that. You'll be out of the water for a while."

"You mean really out—not like in a cave?" Sarah demanded.

"Yes. As I told you, Mount Tor sticks out of the water. It's an old volcano. We'll be able to make our plans about how to get into the Citadel when we get there—if there is any such thing as a plan," he murmured as though to himself.

They pulled their belongings together and mounted the sea beasts. Sarah felt that she had begun to know hers. She was still afraid of him and his huge teeth, but when he nuzzled her she ran her hand over the sandpaperlike skin and said, "You're an ugly thing, but you've been the best thing for me at this time." She slipped into the saddle, thinking how strange it was that she did that as easily as a cowboy would slip into the saddle of a horse. Then when Val led out, she leaned forward to cut down on the water resistance, and the party began their journey.

It was not a long journey, but there was danger. Sarah

—and she was sure all the others—kept her eyes moving constantly, and Val kept leading them through small canyons and behind reefs, out of the open water. At last he turned and waved his arm forward, saying, "There it is. There are the foothills of Mount Tor."

Sarah looked forward eagerly and saw that the ocean floor was giving way to small rises. As they moved forward, she saw that it was a mountain indeed. It rose steeply out of the water, much like a mountain Sarah had once climbed in Washington State. *But,* she thought, *it's much easier to climb on a sea beast than it is to pull yourself up by your fingernails.*

The water grew clearer and brighter, almost translucent. Then Sarah's shark broke the surface, and she blinked at the brilliance of the sun, almost blinded.

"This way," Val said. "Let's get out of sight."

They all had to cover their eyes until they got accustomed to the beams of the sun, and Val led them to a small harbor that seemed made to order. "We can keep our beasts here," he said, "until we decide what to do."

"We'll have to feed them," Wash said, as he patted his shark on the side. "Don't want anything to happen to these fellows." They had brought special food, concentrated fish cakes, and it was amusing to see how the sharks took them into their huge maws.

Their teeth could have torn a horse in two, Sarah noted, but the beasts were as gentle as the porpoises and offered no harm.

As they left the lagoon, Val said, "You can take off your suits now. We'll store all of our equipment here."

Soon they were free of the diving uniforms and were walking around in their green, fish-scale swimsuits, enjoying the sunshine and the warm breeze.

"Now, this is something," Reb said. "It's almost as pretty here as it is in Texas."

Sarah agreed. "I didn't realize how much I missed the world up here."

Dave chipped in, "Yeah, I feel like I'm waterlogged." He looked back at the sea. "It'll be hard to go down there again."

Val laughed. "You're not real mariners. But I guess you have to be born in it to really know what it's like. Come on," he said, "let's see what is here. I've been here only once, and then we just touched the shore."

They moved inland and discovered that the tip of Mount Tor was not large at all, no more than a quarter of a mile across. But there was a large, circular crater right in the center. They came to it cautiously and peered down into the darkness.

"It's an old volcano, all right," Jake said. "Sure hope it don't decide to go off until we get away from here."

Abbey said, "I'm hungry. Can't we make a fire? Are we going to stay here all night?"

Her words spurred them on, and darkness was falling. By the time it was completely dark, they had found firewood and a brisk, cheerful blaze dotted the darkness.

"Aren't you afraid somebody will see our fire—some of the outposts?" Josh asked Val.

"I don't think so. My people don't think about above-the-surface very much. They'd be looking for us down below."

"Well, that's a good thing," Josh said. "I'm all tensed up, expecting to see some of those mariners any minute."

"You'll see them tomorrow, or whenever we decide to make our try," Val said grimly. Then he looked around. "Here's the situation." He drew a map in the dirt. "Here's where we are, on top of Mount Tor. Over there, to the north and to the east a little bit, is the Citadel of Neptune."

"How far is it?" Josh demanded.

"Not far, maybe three miles. Between here and there are half a dozen outposts, but the mariners don't stay in them much. They're out parading back and forth, so they've got a chain that surrounds the Citadel, just like we do with Atlantis."

They stared at the crude map he had drawn, and they talked a long time about some way to get in.

"How many gates are there?" Sarah asked.

"Well, that's the bad news. There's only one, and you can bet it's guarded like nothing you've ever seen before."

"Then I think we ought to try to sneak in when they're changing the guards," Josh suggested.

"That might work to get us to the gate," Val objected, "but it wouldn't get us through the gate."

They talked for a while more, and Val at last said, "I've thought all the while this was a wild scheme. I never really thought we'd get this far, but now it looks like it's all hopeless."

Sarah smiled at him. "You'll think of something."

Josh frowned at that and got up and walked off.

Sarah saw his movement and found an excuse to leave too. She caught up with him as he walked around the circle of fire, staring up at the stars. "What's wrong with you, Josh?"

"Nothing."

"You think I don't know you better than that?"

"Maybe you don't know me as well as you think."

"I know you well enough to know that you're jealous."

"Jealous? You always think that! You thought it about Abbey. You think I don't do anything but walk around making ga-ga eyes at you?"

"Please, Josh, don't be angry. After all, Val has brought us this far."

"Well, a lot of good that does." He snorted. "If we can't get in, what good does it do to be here?"

"Something will come up," she pleaded. "It'll be all right."

Josh continued to argue bitterly, and finally Sarah snapped, "What is it with you, Josh? You always have to be the great leader, the one that makes all the decisions?" Instantly she was sorry, for she knew that Josh had been forced into many situations where he had had to prove his courage. She knew also that if it hadn't been for him, they would have all been lost long ago.

Quickly she opened her mouth to apologize, but he said shortly, "Think whatever you please," then whirled and disappeared into the darkness.

"Josh—Josh!" she cried out. But the only sound was the echo of her voice. Slowly she turned and went back. She sat down beside the campfire.

Val looked over at her. "Your boyfriend mad at me?"

"He's not my boyfriend."

Val grinned, his teeth very white in the reflection of the fire. "Well, he thinks he is. Don't worry, he'll be all right." Then he looked around at the Sleepers and said, "Look, we've accomplished one thing. We've discovered we can get within striking distance of the Citadel. Now, here's my plan. I'll go back to Atlantis, and you all wait here. I'll bring a force back—a small army—and we'll wait till the gate is least protected." His eyes gleamed in the darkness. "Then we'll fall on them and force the gate."

Sarah stirred nervously. "That's not what Goel said, though. He told us to see Aramis in person, not start a war."

Val shrugged. "How would you see Aramis if you couldn't get inside?"

Sarah said suddenly, "We could just go right up to the

gate. We'd be prisoners, but surely we'd get to see the admiral."

"Don't bet on that," Val snapped angrily. "Aramis used to be a man of honor, but something happened to him. You can't trust anything he says anymore."

"Well, I'm against your going," Dave said. "Let's wait till tomorrow. Maybe something will come up."

Val stared. "All right. Till tomorrow then."

* * *

Morning came, and they had breakfast.

Wash said, "That's about all the food we've got."

But Sarah was not thinking of food. Josh was still gone, and she said, "I'm worried about Josh. We'll have to go look for him."

Val shrugged carelessly. "Nothing much can happen to him on this island—it's such a small place. He's just out there somewhere nursing his feelings, but he'll come in when he gets hungry enough."

This did not satisfy Sarah.

They waited for half an hour, and suddenly Abbey cried, "Look, there he is. There comes Josh."

Sarah looked up, a feeling of relief in her heart. She saw Josh step over the crest of a hill and walk rapidly toward them. She ran to him before anyone else could get there, saying, "Josh, I'm sorry about what I said."

He smiled at her, and there was a light in his eyes that had not been there the previous night. "It's OK. Things are going to be all right."

By that time the others had come up, surrounding him.

He repeated, "We're all right—I think." He looked at Val. "That crater—did you know there's a ladder down it, right down inside? When you get to the bottom, there's a tunnel, and it's headed northeast, right toward the Citadel."

Val opened his mouth, closed it, and then straightened up. "That may be it," he said excitedly. "It could be an escape tunnel that Aramis had built so that if things got too bad in the Citadel, they could come through the tunnel and make their escape through Mount Tor. Let's go look."

* * *

At the crater's edge they peered down into blackness.

"Here's the ladder, see. And it goes down a long way. Nearly pulled my arms out coming back up."

"It's dark down there," Val said. "How did you see?"

"Well, it's dark most of the way, but when you get down to the tunnel, there are some kind of lights in the side, not lights exactly but luminous stuff. Kind of a greenish glow. Enough to see by, not much more."

Val grunted. "That would be the smart way to build a tunnel—put luminous rock in the sides of it so there'd be no lights to burn out." He stared around him, then looked at Josh. He put out his hand and said, "I was too sharp with you, young fellow. It looks like you found the way."

Josh flushed, then took Val's hand. "Well, I'm glad things look a little better."

Val said, "We'll have to plan well. I've got to make a map of the Citadel. I was there twice, and I can remember most of how it's built. Once we're inside, we still have to get to Aramis."

Josh said, "Good idea. And all of us need to know as much as we can about what to do when we get inside. You make the map, and we'll all study it."

"I'll do that, and then I'll just make a reconnaissance. One of us ought to go through and find out for sure where

117

the tunnel goes and see if it's guarded. The rest of you can study the map while I check it out."

"Oh, Val, Val, that could be dangerous."

Val grinned at Sarah. "I don't think so. I think we'll find that at the end of the tunnel there's a door, and we can walk right into the Citadel. But we need to check first."

Val drew the map, armed himself, and with a wave said, "I'll be back as soon as I can. We may have to move fast, so everyone be ready." Then he turned and left for the crater.

When he was gone, Jake said, "You're a pretty smart fellow, Josh. How'd you know there's a tunnel down at the bottom of that crater?"

"I didn't know. I was just crazy enough to try anything, so when I saw that ladder, I knew I had to go down it."

"We're lucky to have you with us." Jake grinned. "It takes a smart fellow to figure out a thing like that."

"I'm not very smart, Jake, and we're not inside yet, so let's all keep on saying our prayers."

Sarah smiled at him. "I'm proud of you, Josh. You did fine."

Josh's face burned, and he merely mumbled and turned away. He was thinking now about the tunnel and what lay at the end of it. Perhaps as all the rest of them were thinking, he wondered what they would actually do in the Citadel with a thousand different passageways.

He thought, *Goel will have to be with us, or we'll never get there.*

14
Betrayed

The tunnel that led underneath the ocean floor was cut out of solid rock. As they moved slowly along, weapons at ready, Val marveled at it. "It must have taken a long time to cut a tunnel like this. Lots of work. But it makes an excellent escape route."

"What about our beasts?" Sarah asked. "What will happen to them if we don't get back?"

Val smiled down at her, his eyes glowing as a reflection of the pale luminosity of the rocks. "Don't worry. They're trained to eventually go back to the base of Atlantis. They'll be all right."

The tunnel itself was no more than six feet high and wide enough for only two people, at the most, to squeeze through at one time. It made Sarah nervous to be walking steadily into what could be the lion's mouth, and she asked, "Val, do you think we can find Aramis? I mean, that's a busy place, isn't it, the Citadel?"

"Yes, it is. It's a honeycomb of tunnels, passageways, rooms, a city in itself. But we'll find him." He smiled down at her. "I don't want you to worry, Sarah. Things are going to be all right."

Sarah smiled too. "I feel safe with you to lead us, Val."

Val lost his smile for a moment. "You really trust people, don't you, Sarah?"

"Yes, don't you?"

Val shook his head. "It's not the way of the world.

I've been brought up mostly to trust myself. That's the way it is with royalty."

"Uneasy lies the head that wears the crown?" she asked.

He stared at her. "That's the way it is. What made you say a thing like that?"

"Oh, that's just a line from a play written by a man called Shakespeare a long time ago."

"He knew about kings, all right. When you're in line for the throne, everyone either wants to kill you or to get you to do what they want you to do. 'Uneasy lies the head that wears the crown,'" he repeated. "That's the way it is."

They walked on for what seemed hours, and then Val held up his hand. "The door is just up ahead."

"Did you open it when you were here checking it out, Val?" Sarah asked.

"Oh, yes. And there are no guards on the other side. Our only problem, if we get through it, will be to find Aramis alone." He looked at them. "You know, all these spear guns won't help us a bit. There are a thousand guards in there, and we can't fight all of them."

"What do you think we ought to do?" Josh asked.

Val said, "I think we'd better go as quietly as we can, and these things make a lot of noise clanking around. We'll leave them out in the tunnel, then when we come back we can pick them up again."

Even as he spoke, they reached a large door that seemed to be made of heavy metal or glass. "Just pile them here," Val said and stripped off his own spear gun and dagger. "We may need them when we come back through."

Josh said, "I don't like this idea. We may meet just one man . . ."

"Well, that's up to the group, of course," Val said.

"But I know that right now it's more important to be quiet than it is to have a useless spear gun."

Sarah put her hand on Josh's arm. "Please, let's do what he says, Josh. After all, you can't fight a thousand men."

Slowly Josh turned to her, then shrugged. "All right," he said quietly. He stripped off his quiver of darts and spears and laid it down with his spear gun beside the wall.

When the rest of them had done the same, Val said, "All right. You all remember the map. We go in, and we follow the map that I laid down. That will take us right to Aramis's private quarters. We'll just have to hope we don't meet any guards. If we do, we'll have to hide."

"Doesn't sound too promising to me," Jake said. "If there's a thousand men in there, how're we going to dodge all of them?"

"Well, Aramis's quarters aren't very far." Val thought a moment. "Instead of all of us trying to get through, why don't we do this? You wait in the storeroom on the other side of this door. You should be safe there. And I'll go get Aramis."

"Why, he wouldn't come for you, would he?"

"He might. After all, we know each other, and he might listen long enough to hear what I have to say. I don't think all eight of us can move down these halls without being seen. But I could pass for one of Aramis's men. There are so many, they wouldn't know one more mariner. I think I could bluff my way through."

He talked rapidly, and in the end Sarah said, "It sounds right to me. Are we all for it?"

She saw most of them nodding, but Josh said nothing at all. Disappointed, she said, "Most of us are for it. Take us inside, Val."

"All right. Now be very quiet." He moved forward,

turned the handle, and the door swung smoothly back on its hinges.

Light flooded into the dark tunnel, and Sarah blinked against the brightness. They entered a large room, at least thirty feet long and twenty feet in breadth.

Val shut the door and came back to whisper, "There's the door that leads inside. You wait here and don't make any noise until I get back."

Sarah put her hand on his arm. "We'll be asking Goel to help you, Val."

He nodded briefly, then left without another word.

Sarah and the other Sleepers looked around the room. It was bare except for a few tables and chairs and several storage compartments that mostly stood empty.

When they had explored, they all sat down, except for Reb. "I'm nervous," he said, pacing back and forth. "Never did like waiting."

Josh said heavily, "You might as well sit down. It may take a long time."

Sarah sat beside Josh. He did not meet her gaze. Finally, speaking so quietly that the others could not hear, she said, "Josh, I wish we were like we used to be."

"I guess you can't go back again and be what you were."

"Of course you can! Good friends can. Even though we don't agree, we're not enemies, are we, Josh?"

He looked at her. "No, we could never be that. We've been through too much together." He suddenly reached out awkwardly and patted her shoulder. "You know how much I think of you, Sarah, and always have."

Tears burned her eyes. She captured his hand and pressed it against her shoulder. "Thank you, Josh. I needed to hear something like that."

There was nothing to do, and when there is nothing to do, time crawls by. No one had a watch, and they were too nervous to do much talking. After a long time, Josh said, "Listen. Do you hear anything?"

Instantly, they all came to their feet, their heads cocked toward the door.

"I think I hear somebody coming," Wash said.

"I hope it's Aramis," Abbey said. "What will we do if it's some guards?"

"We'll have to try to jump them," Josh said. "Dave, you and Jake and Wash and I—if it's just two—will take one apiece."

"OK." The boys got ready on each side of the door, ready to jump.

The door swung open.

Sarah, who was standing in the middle of the room, blinked and raised her hand to her mouth in shock.

Val entered and with him a tall man wearing a dark green cape. Behind them stood at least twenty armed mariners, spear guns at ready.

Val turned to the tall man. "Here they are, Duke Lenomar. Remember our agreement."

Duke Lenomar, tall and somehow threatening-looking, ran his dark eyes over the Sleepers. He seemed to pay little attention to Val's words and murmured absently, "Oh yes, our agreement."

Sarah said, "This isn't Aramis, is it?"

Duke Lenomar laughed aloud. "No, my dear young lady, I am Duke Lenomar, adviser to Aramis."

All eyes went to Val, who suddenly flushed. "Look, I can explain all this."

"How can you explain bringing these guards?" Josh demanded.

Val tried to explain, the words tumbling out of his mouth. "Nothing else would have worked. Don't you see that? We have to make an arrangement with Aramis, and the only way to do that is through Duke Lenomar."

"That wasn't what Goel told us to do," Sarah said sharply, tears in her eyes. "You betrayed us, Val, after we trusted you."

Val came at once to stand beside her and put his hand on her arm. He spoke rapidly. "You have to look at it this way—we're fighting for our lives here. Whatever we do is done for Atlantis."

One look around the room showed Sarah that the others were staring at Val with dismay.

At that moment there came the sound of footsteps, and a tall, blond man wearing a green robe and a gold medallion stepped into the room. Without being told, Sarah knew this was Lord Admiral Aramis.

He stopped inside the door, and Duke Lenomar said, "We have captured the Sleepers, my lord, just as I told you."

Aramis looked carefully at the Sleepers. Sarah felt, as his bright blue eyes bored into her, that Aramis was looking deep inside her heart. But she met his gaze boldly, without blinking.

Finally Aramis said, "Well, Valar, we meet again."

Valar at once went on his knees before Aramis. "I have come to join you, sire."

Aramis looked down at the young man. "What about your king?"

"Like yourself, Lord Aramis, I am forced to choose between my love for him and survival for Atlantis, for I realize, as you tried to tell us long ago, we must join ourselves to the strongest force."

Aramis stared at him, then looked back at the Sleepers. "We will speak of this. Come with me, Valar."

Lenomar stepped forward, saying, "We must do away with the Sleepers!"

Aramis whirled and glared at his lieutenant. "No, let them live. Keep them under close guard."

"Your Majesty, we must—"

"Those are my orders, Lenomar." Aramis glared even more fiercely. "If anything happens to them, I will hold you accountable."

Lenomar looked dismayed as Aramis walked away. Then he rested his eyes on the Sleepers and said to the guards, "Take them to the cells."

The young people were taken, each with a guard on either side, to a compartment large enough for all of them. There were separate cells for sleeping.

Lenomar's eyes were cruel as he said, "I know who you are, the servants of Goel."

"Yes," Sarah said at once, and Josh spoke at the same time.

They glanced at each other, and Josh went on. "We *are* the servants of Goel, and I can tell that you are the servant of the Dark Power."

Lenomar whispered, "Perhaps you will carry that secret to your grave." He then walked out, and the Sleepers were left alone.

Sarah moved to a chair, fell into it, put her arms on the table, and then buried her face against them. Sobs shook her body.

At last Josh came over and touched her shoulder and said, "Don't do that, Sarah."

"I can't help it. It was all my fault."

"We're not blaming you."

Sarah lifted her head. Tears ran down her face. "It's all my fault! Yes, it is, because I . . . I . . . ."

"What is it, Sarah? What's the matter?" Josh asked. "It'll be all right. We're just doing what Goel told us to do."

Sarah's voice trembled and became a whisper. "But Josh, I lied about what Goel said."

"You did what?" Dave demanded, and the others looked at her with shock. "How did you lie?"

Sarah looked around. "It was all true except one thing." She bowed her head and bit her lip and tried to restrain a sob. "It was all true except what I said about Valar. Goel didn't tell me to bring him."

"Why did you do it then, Sarah?" Abbey asked.

"Oh, I don't know, Abbey. Why do I do crazy things, anyway? I guess I liked him, I trusted him, and—" she raised a hand to her mouth "oh, now I know!"

"What is it?" Josh asked.

"Do you remember before we left the mountain, the last time we saw Goel? Do you remember what he did?"

Josh nodded. "He gave each of us some kind of message—prediction, you might say." His eyes lighted up. "Oh. I guess now you understand—" He broke off and looked down at his hands, apparently not knowing what more to say.

It was Sarah who spoke. "I had forgotten what he said to me, but now I remember, just like he was saying it. He said, 'Daughter, your role will be lonely. Those you trust most will betray you.' You remember he said that to me, and I've done exactly that. I trusted Valar, and he betrayed me."

As the others stood looking on, she put her head back down on the table, racked by sobs again.

Abbey came over and patted her and whispered encouragement. One by one, each Sleeper came by and gave her words of comfort.

Last of all, Josh came. "Sarah, I want you to know one thing—well, two things really." He waited until she lifted her head. "First of all, none of us hates you for the mistake you made. Any of us could have done it. We all love you as much as ever."

"Do you, Josh? I don't see how you can," she said in despair.

Then Josh said, "The second thing is, do you think we're better or more loving than Goel?"

"Why, no. Nobody is," Sarah said in surprise.

"Then if we're willing to love you and forgive you, in spite of the mistake, don't you know that he will be?"

Shock ran through Sarah, and somehow a ray of hope came to her. She bit her lip and opened her eyes wide. Then she whispered, "Oh, Josh, do you really think so?"

"I know so." He sat down and put an arm around her. "After all, he's forgiven me for worse."

The two sat there together for a long time, and finally Sarah began to feel that Josh had spoken the truth. Still, there was sadness in her heart. "To think that Goel could have warned me so plainly, and I just ignored the warning."

"Well, that's the way it is with us human beings," Josh said. "We make mistakes. We must trust Goel to get us through despite them."

What must have been less than two hours later, the door opened, and Duke Lenomar came in. "I've come to tell you you have forty-eight hours to make your peace with whatever god you serve, for in exactly two days, at this hour, you will be put to death. It will not be an unpleasant death—at least not a long death."

"What's going to happen to us?" Wash whispered.

"Oh, our method of execution is fairly merciful, I think." Lenomar's thin lips smiled. "We have some hungry sharks that we keep in a tank. Traitors and rebels and heretics are thrown to them as an offering to our god. You will make a fine offering. The Seven Sleepers, an offering to the Dark Lord!" He laughed, then turned and slammed the door.

The seven looked at each other. The door's hollow, clanging sound reminded Sarah of a funeral bell.

15
Perilous Journey

The voice seemed to come from very far away. At first it was so faint that Sarah barely hear it. It came out of the quietness, somehow, disturbing her sleep. Finally she recognized that someone was calling her name.

Sarah. Sarah!

Sarah squirmed in the chair where she had fallen asleep. She tried to close her consciousness, for sleep was a refuge. When she was awake, all she had been able to think about was the shark tank where Duke Lenomar had promised they would be thrown. In sleep, she was at least unaware of that.

Sarah. You must wake, Sarah.

The voice was louder this time, more insistent, and with a start Sarah pulled herself out of deep sleep. She was still groggy, but she had more of her mind about her now. She saw that everyone else had fallen into at least a fitful sleep. She wished she could join them. But as she closed her eyes, the voice came once more, and this time she could not ignore it.

Are you awake, my Sarah? Do you recognize me?

"Goel," Sarah whispered inaudibly. "Is that you, Goel?"

Yes, it is I. Listen carefully, Sarah, for I have a difficult task indeed for anyone to perform.

Sarah's heart sank, for she knew some of the hard things that Goel demanded. But she had also learned what it meant to disobey, and that came to her mind now. She whispered, "Oh, Goel, I lied about your message. I was wrong about Valar. It was my stubbornness and my pride. I'm so sorry."

I know that, my Sarah, and I forgive you. I believe you have learned through this to trust me. Have you not?

"Oh yes, Goel," Sarah said thankfully. A burden seemed lifted from her now that she had been forgiven.

That is good, the voice said. It was a warm voice, full of hope and cheer, strong and steadfast, and as long as she heard it there was no fear at all in her.

Listen carefully now, Goel went on to say, *for upon your obedience depends the fate of many things, the lives of your friends for one.*

Sarah whispered, "Oh, tell me, Goel. I'll do anything."

For the next few minutes she sat still. Those in the room, had they been awake, would have heard no voice, but it came to Sarah as clear as any spoken word she had ever heard. She sat bolt upright, and as the voice went on, her eyes sprang open with shock.

At last Goel said, *Have you understood my commands, Sarah?*

Sarah swallowed hard and said, "Yes, Goel. I will do it, no matter what happens."

There's my fine Sarah. Goel sounded pleased. *Remember, never take counsel of your fears. Remember the promise—I will be with you and keep you safe. Even under the deep. I am there as well as I am under the open sky. Go now, Sarah, and obey my command.*

The voice faded away, and Sarah sat there, every bit of sleep driven from her. Slowly she arose and looked over at the other Sleepers. She wanted to speak to them, but could not, for Goel had commanded otherwise. *This is something you must do alone, Sarah.*

She stepped to the door of the prison, put her hand on the bar, and pulled. She was not surprised when it swung soundlessly open, for so Goel had said. Stepping outside, she drew the door to and noticed that the guards on each side were staring straight ahead, completely motionless, as if they were frozen in position.

Quickly she went down the corridor, passing through two more doors, and at each point the guards stood in that strange frozen attitude.

She reached the door to the holding room, which the tunnel entered, opened it, stepped inside. Without hesitation, she opened the door to the tunnel, went through, and closed it behind her.

The light green fluorescence glowed around her, but Sarah did not wait to think or to look. She hurried forward and did not stop until she had reached the mouth of the lower part of the volcano.

She grasped the edge of the ladder and looked up. It seemed a million miles to the top, and she was already exhausted. Still, she remembered the words of Goel and began to climb. By the time she reached the top and threw herself on the ground, she was completely winded and had to sit there for several minutes until she caught her breath.

Then Sarah climbed to her feet and walked steadily to the campsite. Once there, she removed her diving suit from the case, put it on, and walked out into the water. The sea beasts were gone, and she remember Val's words, "They're trained to eventually go back to the base in Atlantis."

She stood waiting, for Goel had promised that she would be taken from this place. Soon a fin cut through the water, and there before her was a large killer whale. He was so huge that she could not comprehend his size, but somehow she felt no fear as he stopped beside her. There was a saddle on his back, and she immediately mounted the huge beast, grabbed the leather strap in front, and bent forward.

Without a word of command, the beast plunged ahead. He was much faster than any shark, and he knifed through the water, leaving his fin high so that Sarah was not underwater for most of the time. As she sped along, she thought, *This might be fun if it weren't so deadly serious.* The sea beast plunged on through the green waters, and she began to whisper, "Oh, help me to help my friends."

* * *

Princess Jere was a light sleeper, and the instant she heard the sound at her door, she was off her bed like a cat. Snatching up the dagger that was always on her bedside table, she moved quickly across the room and flattened her body against the wall. The door opened slowly, throwing a bar of light across the floor—and someone's shadow. Princess Jere waited until the figure stepped inside, then she leaped upon it, throwing her arm around its throat, and raising her dagger to strike.

A choked voice said, "No, Princess, it's me—Sarah."

Princess Jere withheld the stroke, whirled the girl around, and stared into her face. "It *is* you." Her eyes were hard. Jere shut the door and dragged the girl across the room. She lit a light and faced her, crying angrily, "What have you come back for? To betray us again?"

Sarah said hoarsely, "No, Princess, we never betrayed you."

"Everyone knows what you did," Jere said. "You left with Valar, and you have gone over to the enemy."

Quickly Sarah began pleading. She was trembling. Her hair was wet and stiff with sea water, and somehow she brought a sense of vulnerability. She began by saying, "We left at the bidding of Goel," and she repeated the story of how they had left. She also told how she had dis-obeyed Goel and taken Valar along, deceiving the others.

"I was wrong," she said, as tears came to her eyes. "I disobeyed the voice of Goel, and I put my friends in danger of their lives, and now they're captives, and they will all die unless . . ."

Jere waited for her to continue, and when she did not, said, "Unless what?"

Sarah swallowed hard. She managed to say, "Unless you will go back with me, Princess Jere, they all will per-ish. I, too, for I will go back to be with them."

Jere stared at her. "Have you gone crazy? I, go with you to the Citadel? Do you realize what would happen if I were captured? Aramis would have the perfect hostage. He would take the kingdom, for my father would give it up for my life."

"Yes, I know that."

Jere, for the next twenty minutes, shot questions at Sarah, trying to trip her up in her story, but she could not. Finally she said grudgingly, "I think you're telling me the truth, or part of it, but I don't understand the rest. Why should I go with you to the Citadel? What can *I* do?"

"No military might can overcome Aramis, but there is a power greater than that."

Jere blinked. "What power?"

"The power of love, my lady," Sarah said quietly.

"What—what do you mean by that?"

"I mean that you love the Lord Aramis."

"No, I do not. How could I love a traitor?"

"You know what he was better than anyone," Sarah said quickly. "Everyone speaks of what a wonderful man he was, how kind and gentle and courageous, everything a man should be."

Jere bit her lip. "Yes, I did love him, but no more. I cannot love a traitor."

"My lady, you know he is not himself. There is a man called Duke Lenomar. He has clouded the mind of the Lord Aramis."

"Lenomar." Jere stared, then whispered. "I knew it. I never trusted that man. Aramis and I had quarrels over him. But Aramis couldn't see through him. What has Lenomar done?"

"Somehow he has influenced Lord Aramis, and only you, I think, can bring him to himself."

After a long time, Jere's shoulders slumped, and she said, "I will go with you. My life is empty without him anyway. At least I will see him once more."

16

Strongest Force of All

I still say it's some kind of trick that Duke Lenomar is playing on us. Where else could she have gone?"

The captives had been arguing about Sarah's abrupt and mysterious disappearance. Dave maintained stubbornly that it was some trick on the part of the duke.

Josh rubbed his chin nervously. Ever since he had awakened to find Sarah gone, he had not slept. Worry had drawn his face, and now he said, "Well, you may be right, Dave—but I don't see what good that would do him. He's got us where he wants us anyhow."

Dave said quickly, "But he wants to know more about Goel. We know that for sure."

Wash shook his head. "Any more of these questionings, and I'm not sure I can hold up. They keep asking the same things over and over again."

Lenomar had taken the Sleepers, one by one, from their common cell into a smaller room, where for what seemed like hours he had interrogated them, asking question after question about their activities since emerging from the sleep capsules. Mostly he asked about Goel and his plans.

At the end of one session, Josh had stared at the tall, sinister-looking duke and said, "Goel doesn't let me in on all of his plans, but I know one thing he has on his mind."

"Ah, and what is that, my young friend?"

"To put people like you and the Dark Lord out of business," Josh had said defiantly.

Lenomar glared, and for one moment Josh knew fear.

But then Lenomar had merely motioned to his guard. "Take him back with the others."

And now the group talked nervously about Sarah, but there seemed nothing anyone could do.

* * *

The Sleepers waited, and time dragged on.

"I'm so afraid, Dave," Abbey said. "I can't stand the thought of that awful—that awful—"

It was clear to Dave that she couldn't bring the words *shark tank* to her lips. She was very pale. Her lips trembled, and she whispered, "I never was very strong."

Dave tried to put a good front on the situation, although he too felt something in the pit of his stomach. "Don't give up, Abbey. It's not over till it's over. Goel will come through for us."

Abbey looked up at him, biting her lip. "Do you remember back when Goel talked to all of us and gave those—prophecies?"

"I remember. I remember what he said to me," Dave said ruefully. "That I'd have the hardest task of any of us. But I don't see that this is any harder for me than for any of the rest of you." He brightened. "Say, Abbey, if I'm going to have to do a hard task, and it's harder than anybody else's, why then that means we'll get out of here. Because here, nothing's harder for anybody—it's all the same."

Abbey brightened too for a moment, but then a cloud passed over her face and she dropped her head. "Do you remember what Goel asked me?" Without waiting for an answer, she went on. "He asked me if I'd give up everything for him, and when I said yes, he asked me, 'What about your good looks?'"

"I remember," Dave said. He remembered also that Abbey had said, 'No, I can't do that.'"

"I wish I hadn't said what I did to him. What good is it to look nice when you're going to die? At least, if I had said yes, I'd be ready to go, I think."

Dave suddenly saw how small and vulnerable the girl was. He moved over, put an arm around her, and gave her a companionable squeeze. "We can't give up," he said. "I've been thinking Josh is right. Sarah hasn't gone over to the enemy—I know that, so something's going on. We just have to keep our hopes up."

* * *

Jake and Reb agreed with Josh about Sarah, but as time wore on, Wash grew more and more tense and apprehensive. None of them spoke of the specifics of the execution, but he knew they were all high-strung.

"I sometimes wonder why I was ever picked for this job," Jake said. "Doesn't seem like I add much to the group."

Reb said, "I don't think any of us adds much, but it's the group that's important."

Wash agreed. "I think that's right, Reb. And somehow us Sleepers have got more to do than die in a shark tank." Then he realized what he had said. "Sorry, didn't mean to get too specific."

Hours passed, and they all seemed to grow more and more tense.

* * *

Finally, steps sounded outside the door, and the bolt clanged metallically as it was withdrawn. The door swung open, and the chief guard stepped inside. Behind him stood a squad of heavily armed mariners. The guard's face was emotionless, but he said, "I'm sorry. It's time now."

Josh looked up at him. "You're sorry? I don't think you really mean that."

137

A strange expression crossed the chief guard's face, "Believe it or not," he said quietly, "I *am* sorry. My brother is one of the mariners whose life you spared." He lowered his voice, perhaps so the other guards could not hear. "And I am not the only one. Many of our people feel that Duke Lenomar is wrong."

"What about Lord Aramis?" Josh asked quickly.

The guard shook his head briefly. "I cannot say." He hesitated and then said, "But I cannot offer you any hope. He is under the control of Duke Lenomar, it seems." Then he stiffened, and his lips grew thin. Lifting his voice he said, "Come this way."

The tall, strong guards formed a double line, and the Sleepers took their places between them. As they walked down the long corridor, their footsteps rang with a hollow sound.

When Josh looked around, he saw that Dave's face was pale and knew that his own must look the same. Abbey stumbled, and he moved quickly to take her arm. He said, "I've felt better in my life, but one thing I'm going to do—show Lenomar that some people are not afraid of death."

His words caught the attention of the chief guard, who turned to look at him, nodding slightly as if in approval. The other Sleepers glanced at Josh, who managed a brief smile.

In what seemed a very short time, they wound through several corridors until finally they came to double doors, which two of the guards opened.

The chief guard said, "Step inside."

Once inside, Josh saw this was the largest room that they had encountered in the Citadel. It was built like an amphitheater, and there were seats rising slightly around the outside. In the center stood a large tank some fifty feet across, at least. As Josh was marched along with the others, closer to the tank, he saw dark bodies moving restlessly beneath the surface of the water.

"Don't look at that, Abbey," he said. "Just keep thinking of Goel."

At one side of the tank, a group of important-looking individuals occupied a row of raised seats. In front of them sat the Lord High Admiral Aramis and, beside him, Duke Lenomar. The chief guard halted, looking up at the two men. "Sire, we have brought the prisoners."

Aramis's eyes met those of Josh.

There is, Josh thought, *something strange about his face.* His countenance, handsome though it was, was somehow marred with confusion, especially his eyes. Their eyes locked, and a long silence fell over the group as everyone waited for Aramis to speak.

Slowly the admiral stood to his feet, looked down at the captives, then said, as if to himself, "These are very small enemies for a man such as I. And very young."

Immediately Duke Lenomar said, "Young and small, but still they are the servants of the enemy. They have all confessed that they are in the service of the one called Goel, who seeks to ruin us all."

Aramis blinked. His eyes went from one to another of the small group. "Does the Lord High Admiral make war on children?" he asked.

Again Duke Lenomar spoke up quickly. "You must not think of them as children. They are small and young, but they have in them the poison that will destroy us." He whispered, "No one likes to see young lives destroyed, but that is the price of winning the kingdom, my lord. Now, you must give the command."

Aramis seemed not to be listening, for his eyes were locked on those of Josh again. He considered the boy, then said, "Do you have anything to say?"

Josh lifted his voice, and he lifted his hand, his fist

clenched, "Long live King Cosmos! Long live the kingdom of Atlantis! And long live the House of Goel!"

His words rang through the hall. And as Josh glanced about the room, he saw that many of the guards and the mariners who sat in the seats seemed to be moved by them. He thought, *Some of these people are not against us. It's that Duke Lenomar—he's the one who wants us to die.*

Aramis said, "You speak of Goel."

"Yes," Josh said, and then something came into his mind. He lowered his voice so that it was quiet but strong. "And may the peace of Goel come to you, Lord Aramis."

This time there was an audible response from the leaders, and Lenomar looked around, obviously seeing that the young man's words had swayed even some of them. He called out, "Into the tank with them!"

Aramis at once whirled, his eyes wide with anger. "Have you become my commander, Lenomar?"

"Why, no, sire, of course not. I beg your pardon, sire, but my anxiety for you and for the kingdom made me speak unadvisedly. I await your command."

Aramis stared at the duke for a long time, started to speak, then turned back to the captives. There was a weighty silence before, finally, Aramis said, "I have never turned my back on my enemies in battle. No man has ever called me a coward. I have fought the battle of the king faithfully until—" he hesitated "—until . . ." He could not finish his sentence.

Then he seemed to find a new thought. "You young people are victims in a war not of your making. You are young, but there will be others—many, though older than yourselves—who will suffer in this terrible conflict. That is the way of war—the innocent suffer." He stopped and looked thoughtful. "I would that it were not so. I would that you could escape the fate that you have brought upon yourselves."

Suddenly a cry rang out, "Goel bless Lord Admiral Aramis!"

A murmur traveled around the room and suddenly swelled into a babble of voices, for a figure from nowhere stepped out into the open space just behind the Sleepers.

A voice cried out, "It's the Princess Jere!"

Many of the watching mariners had spent their lives serving King Cosmos, Josh realized. They knew Jere well. They had sworn their loyalty to the house of Cosmos, and here stood its living representative. Many of those around the room now stood, fully half the number, and someone cried out, "Hail, Princess Jere." The cry was taken up by others.

As for Aramis, his face had gone pale when he saw the shapely young woman who stood looking fearlessly up at him. "Jere," he whispered.

Lenomar turned to his lieutenant. "Get ready to give the signal," he hissed. "This is getting out of hand. When I give the word, kill Aramis and be sure the princess does not survive."

"Aye, my lord." Josh watched the lieutenant fade back and begin to move among his underlings, giving orders.

Aramis continued to stare down at the young woman. He swallowed hard and blinked. Something had apparently come to mind that he could not shake off. At length, in a quiet voice that still carried all through the room, he said, "You know you forfeit your life by coming to this place, Princess Jere."

Jere's hair, rich and thick, glowed in the light from the ceiling, and her eyes were bright and clear. There seemed no fear in her as she answered, "I am aware of that, Lord Aramis."

Aramis seemed like a man only half awake. "I don't understand," he said almost inaudibly. "Why would you do this?"

141

"Because I love Atlantis, even as you love Atlantis, Lord Admiral."

A murmur went around the room once again, and Aramis straightened, seeming to gain his composure. "There was a time," he said, "when you did not believe so."

"Yes, I called you a traitor and a rebel, didn't I, my lord? I did not show, perhaps, what I felt."

"I am still a rebel in the eyes of your father," Aramis said flatly.

"Yes, that is true." Jere stopped then and took a deep breath. "Do you not know that my father still loves you? Even though you have led his kingdom into rebellion? He and my mother love you just the same, even though they grieve over what has happened."

"That cannot be!" Aramis cried out, put his hands to his head, shaking it wildly. "They cannot love me, not after—"

"Yes, they can," Jere said clearly. "They love you, because love doesn't change. It's the same when someone we love is hurt or injured. When they fall, when they make a mistake, we grieve over them, but true love forgives, always forgives."

Aramis dropped his hands. He stepped down from the dais and walked straight to where Jere stood.

Lenomar murmured, "Get ready," and his lieutenant nodded grimly.

Aramis stood before Jere, looked down at her. "And what about you, Princess? Do you still love me—in spite of everything?"

She lifted her head, reached out one hand, and put it on his chest. Her lips trembled, but her eyes were clear and steady. "Yes, Aramis," she whispered. "I have always loved you—and I always shall."

Aramis looked like a man who had been struck. Slowly he reached forward, took her hand, and held it. He looked like a man coming out of some nightmarish experience.

"You're almost free," she whispered. "You've been held in bondage for so long, but do you remember what it was like back when we were one, and you served the king?"

Aramis did appear to remember. He said, "I don't know what came over me. I don't understand." Then he lifted his head and lifted up his voice. "There will be no executions."

No sooner had his command rung out than Lenomar nodded at the lieutenant. "Strike—kill them all!"

A mariner standing close to the edge of the tank lifted his spear gun, aiming it at Aramis.

"Look out!" Josh cried. He had only time to make one leap and knock the admiral to one side.

The dart whistled by Aramis's cheek. Everywhere Lenomar's personal guards and those loyal to him were attacking.

Aramis shouted, "All for King Cosmos and Atlantis—to me!"

Then the most frightful battle began. The sides were evenly matched, and soon the two factions were in a death struggle. Darts from the spear guns of Lenomar's guards whistled, some of them taking down men instantly.

Josh saw a guard rush toward Sarah—one of Lenomar's men, he suspected. Josh snatched up a sword from a fallen mariner, made a wild run, and just as the mariner raised his knife over Sarah's back, Josh shoved by, thrusting. The guard went down, and Josh pulled Sarah back into a place of safety.

Even as they watched the fighting, Josh said, "I don't know how you did it, Sarah—but you did!"

"It was all Goel," she answered. "He did it all. But look—Aramis is rallying his men."

The tide of battle had turned so that Lenomar and his group were being driven back. Lenomar opened his mouth to command, "Kill them—" but a dart caught him in the chest, and he fell.

With Lenomar's death, his supporters lost heart, and soon Aramis had surrounded those who were left. "Put them all under lock and key," he ordered. Then he glanced down at Jere, who had come to stand beside him. "Do not harm them anymore. I've found out that even though a man is wrong, he can change."

Then he said to Jere, "I feel so strange, as if I've been asleep for a long time."

"You *have* been asleep—in a nightmare." She smiled up at him. "Now, it's a new world."

Jere lifted her head, and—despite the hubbub of the guards getting their prisoners together—Aramis, in full view of everyone, leaned forward and kissed her. Then he fell on one knee and raised his sword. "My loyalty," he cried out, "is to the house of Cosmos, the king of Atlantis."

Josh stood with the Sleepers. He said, "Well, I guess that about takes care of this problem, doesn't it? Now, Sarah," he said, "we've got to hear what happened."

Sarah seemed not to be listening. She was watching as Jere leaned forward and raised Aramis. "Isn't that sweet?" she said. "Look, they're so in love."

Josh looked at the couple. "You're so romantic, Sarah. This is a whole kingdom, and you're looking at one man and one woman."

Sarah smiled, then whispered, "That's what the world comes down to, Josh—one man and one woman."

Josh could think of nothing to say. She reached up and took his hand and squeezed it tightly.

17
What Next?

The great banquet hall of the city of Atlantis was filled to capacity. Everywhere, servants brought silver and golden trays filled with food, and golden cups full of drink, to those at the long tables. At one end of the room on a raised dais sat the royalty of the kingdom. King Cosmos sat in the center. On his right was Queen Mab, on his left the Princess Jere, and beside Princess Jere sat Aramis, the Lord High Admiral of Atlantis.

The Seven Sleepers sat at a table at a right angle so that they faced both the royal family and the lords and nobles and citizens of the kingdom. Josh was between Sarah and Dave, and as they laughed and talked, Sarah said, "Look, isn't that romantic? Aramis is holding Jere's hand!"

Josh looked up and grinned. "Well, if he sat any closer to her, he'd be on the other side, wouldn't he? From the look on his face, I guess that's one happy man."

"They're all happy." Sarah nodded. She looked very pretty tonight in the gown that Princess Jere had lent her. It was pale blue with a frothy, matching bodice and skirt. "Look at the king, how proud he is."

"Yes, he's got his family together, and I guess he won't have to worry about the next ruler, will he?"

Dave asked, "I wonder what's going to happen to Valar?"

"Well, he won't be thrown into a shark tank, that's for sure," Josh said.

Sarah looked over to one side where Valar sat silently, his face pale, beside an armed guard. He had lost weight during the days since Aramis had overthrown Duke Lenomar. He had come to the royal court with the group and watched Cosmos and the queen welcome Aramis with open arms. Since then, Valar had been kept under house arrest.

Sarah said suddenly, "I'm going over and speak to him." Quickly she arose, ignoring the eyes that were watching her. One of the seats beside Val was empty, and she slipped into it.

When he looked at her, his face was haggard, and he said, "Come to gloat over me?"

"No, Val," Sarah said quietly.

Val waited for her to speak further. When she said nothing, he stared down at the table, his fists clenched. "You might as well go ahead and say it. You're thinking it—everybody else is—what an ingrate I am, a traitor to the king and queen." He lifted his head and looked at Sarah with misery in his eyes. "And I was a traitor to you too, Sarah. I let you trust me, then I betrayed you." He struggled with words, finally saying, "I'm . . . sorry."

Sarah was filled with pity for the young man. Not caring who saw, she reached over and put her hand on his. When he looked up at her again, startled, she smiled. "We all make mistakes, Val, but you're young, and it's not too late. King Cosmos still loves you, and he'll give you another chance. And the queen, she loves you too."

"I don't know . . . I don't see why they should."

"You can change. Serve the king and Lord Aramis. You'll find out that they're not like Duke Lenomar. They're kind and generous, and before long they'll see that you've changed, that you can be trusted."

He hesitated and blinked. "You—you don't hate me, Sarah? After what I did?"

She squeezed his hand, shaking her head. "I—I believe in you, Val."

A trace of the old humor returned to Val as he said ruefully, "No more king and queen for us though."

"There never was anything like that, Val. You know that. I was just a silly girl." She squeezed his hand again and said, "I must go back now, but remember—learn to trust people and be faithful."

"I will," he said seriously, and he stood to his feet as she rose and crossed the room.

When Sarah got back to her seat, Dave asked, "What did you say to him?"

"Oh, I just told him that he wasn't alone and that we all make mistakes and that he could begin over again."

Dave nodded. "Well, I guess I feel like that now, but I was pretty sore at him."

Josh asked suddenly, "You really mean that, don't you, Sarah?"

She glanced at him in surprise. "Of course. What he did was no worse than what I did. He betrayed me, but I betrayed Goel by being unfaithful. So we're both learning."

Josh said quickly, "All of us are learning."

At that moment, the king called, "The Seven Sleepers, rise and come before the royal throne."

The Sleepers scrambled to their feet and went to stand before King Cosmos. He smiled down at them. "It is a great debt that I owe you seven, and there's no way that I can repay it. You must be content with the gratitude of my queen and myself and my daughter and her fiancé."

He went on to make quite a long speech and said such marvelous things that all of the Sleepers flushed with embarrassment. Finally, Cosmos said, "I trust that you will remain with us for a long time. There is much of our kingdom that you have not seen yet. It would give me pleasure to show you those things."

After the king spoke, there were other speeches,

147

and finally, after many hours of celebrating and feasting, the Sleepers were shown to their suite. It was a large room with separate sleeping compartments, much like their prison, except ornately done. They stepped inside and began to talk excitedly about what had happened.

They were still talking when a voice said, "You have done very well."

They all whirled to see Goel standing beside the door.

"Goel!" Sarah cried. She wanted to run to him but stood where she was, her eyes fixed on him.

"You especially, my daughter, have come through your ordeal very well. I am proud of you. Though you failed me, you are learning."

"Yes, Goel, I'll try my best," Sarah said.

Josh swallowed, for he always felt uneasy in Goel's presence. "Goel, what is next for us? Do we stay here for a while?"

"No, your work is done here. Atlantis is secure. The Dark Lord will not take this part of Nuworld." A frown crossed his face. "But there are other tasks, for the enemy presses hard upon our people."

"You mean, we've got to leave right now?" Jake asked.

"Yes, my son, right now." Then he smiled as he turned to Abbey. "You did not ask where or for what." His smile grew broader. "Is that because you have learned to trust me more than the first time we met?"

"Oh, yes, Goel," Abbey said. Her lips trembled, and she seemed on the verge of tears. "I want so much to do what pleases you."

Goel put out his hand and took Abbey's small one in his. "You are growing up, my daughter," he said softly. "I am pleased with you." Then he looked up. "I am pleased with all of you—but now it is time to go. Gather your things. You may take only what you can carry. We have a long journey, and I have made preparations."

Quickly they scurried around, getting their few things together and changing their banquet finery for work clothes.

"I suppose we'll be traveling under the sea again?" Josh asked. Then a sudden thought came to him. "Will we be seeing Kybus and all the other old friends we lost at the river?"

"I think you might." Goel smiled. "They are in the House of Goel, and all who are there can expect to meet again. Come now. It's just for a little way, but your journey this time will take you far from the ocean."

Goel stepped outside the door. The guards looked at him wide-eyed but did not question him. The Sleepers followed him down the corridors.

Just before they reached the air lock, Sarah was surprised to see Jere emerge from a door. She ran at once to Sarah and pulled her to one side.

After a greeting, Jere said, "You knew I loved Aramis?"

"Well, it was pretty obvious, the way you looked at him." Sarah smiled. "I'm so happy for you."

"This is farewell for a while," Princess Jere said. She kissed Sarah on the cheek and smiled mysteriously. "And I know something about you too."

Sarah looked at her in confusion. "What do you know?"

Jere patted her cheek, then stepped back. "I know what one woman always knows about another woman when she's in love."

Sarah flushed and turned to rejoin the others.

As they headed down the corridor following Goel, Josh fell into step with Sarah. "What did Princess Jere say to you?"

"Oh, just woman talk." She smiled up at him. They went a few steps further, and she said, "You're getting taller. I do like tall men."

Josh blinked like an owl and looked stunned.

Sarah took his arm.

As they followed the others down the corridor to the door that Goel indicated, he said, "Well, I'm glad you like tall fellows—" he grinned "—because there's nothing I can do about that."

"I like you just as you are, Josh."

As they entered the door, Josh looked up at Goel. "I guess we're ready for whatever you have."

Goel smiled again, his lips relaxed. "That is good, my son, for all of you to be one. Come now—I have a task for you!"

Get swept away in the many Gilbert Morris Adventures available from Moody Press:

"Too Smart" Jones
4025-8 Pool Part Thief
4026-6 Buried Jewels
4027-4 Disappearing Dogs
4028-2 Dangerous Woman
4029-0 Stranger in the Cave
4030-4 Cat's Secret
4031-2 Stolen Bicycle
4032-0 Wilderness Mystery

Come along for the adventures and mysteries Juliet "Too Smart" Jones always manages to find. She and her other homeschool friends solve these great adventures and learn biblical truths along the way. Ages 9-14

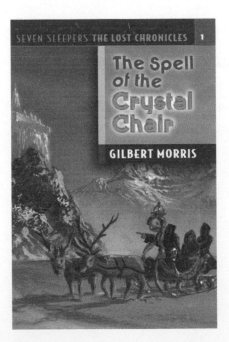

**Seven Sleepers -
The Lost Chronicles**

3667-6 The Spell of the Crystal Chair
3668-4 The Savage Game of Lord Zarak
3669-2 The Strange Creatures of Dr. Korbo
3670-6 City of the Cyborgs

More exciting adventures from the Seven Sleepers. As these exciting young people attempt to faithfully follow Goel, they learn important moral and spiritual lessons. Come along with them as they encounter danger, intrigue, and mystery. Ages 10-14

Dixie Morris Animal Adventures

3363-4 Dixie and Jumbo
3364-2 Dixie and Stripes
3365-0 Dixie and Dolly
3366-9 Dixie and Sandy
3367-7 Dixie and Ivan
3368-5 Dixie and Bandit
3369-3 Dixie and Champ
3370-7 Dixie and Perry
3371-5 Dixie and Blizzard
3382-3 Dixie and Flash

Follow the exciting adventures of this animal lover as she learns more of God and His character through her many adventures underneath the Big Top. Ages 9-14

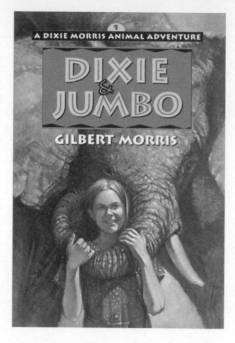

The Daystar Voyages

4102-X Secret of the Planet Makon
4106-8 Wizards of the Galaxy
4107-6 Escape From the Red Comet
4108-4 Dark Spell Over Morlandria
4109-2 Revenge of the Space Pirates
4110-6 Invasion of the Killer Locusts
4111-4 Dangers of the Rainbow Nebula
4112-2 The Frozen Space Pilot

Join the crew of the Daystar as they traverse the wide expanse of space. Adventure and danger abound, but they learn time and again that God is truly the Master of the Universe. Ages 10-14

Seven Sleepers Series

3681-1 Flight of the Eagles
3682-X The Gates of Neptune
3683-3 The Swords of Camelot
3684-6 The Caves That Time Forgot
3685-4 Winged Riders of the Desert
3686-2 Empress of the Underworld
3687-0 Voyage of the Dolphin
3691-9 Attack of the Amazons
3692-7 Escape with the Dream Maker
3693-5 The Final Kingdom

Go with Josh and his friends as they are sent by Goel, their spiritual leader, on dangerous and challenging voyages to conquer the forces of darkness in the new world. Ages 10-14

Bonnets and Bugles Series

0911-3 Drummer Boy at Bull Run
0912-1 Yankee Bells in Dixie
0913-X The Secret of Richmond Manor
0914-8 The Soldier Boy's Discovery
0915-6 Blockade Runner
0916-4 The Gallant Boys of Gettysburg
0917-2 The Battle of Lookout Mountain
0918-0 Encounter at Cold Harbor
0919-9 Fire Over Atlanta
0920-2 Bring the Boys Home

Follow good friends Leah Carter and Jeff Majors as they experience danger, intrigue, compassion, and love in these civil war adventures. Ages 10-14

Moody Press, a ministry of the Moody Bible Institute,
is designed for education, evangelization, and edification.
If we may assist you in knowing more about Christ
and the Christian life, please write us without obligation:
Moody Press, c/o MLM, Chicago, Illinois 60610.